THE YELLOW
WINDMILL

Francis Durbridge

WILLIAMS & WHITING

Cover design by Timo Schroeder

9781915887399

Williams & Whiting (Publishers)
15 Chestnut Grove, Hurstpierpoint,
West Sussex, BN6 9SS

Titles by Francis Durbridge published by Williams & Whiting

1   The Scarf – tv serial
2   Paul Temple and the Curzon Case – radio serial
3   La Boutique – radio serial
4   The Broken Horseshoe – tv serial
5   Three Plays for Radio Volume 1
6   Send for Paul Temple – radio serial
7   A Time of Day – tv serial
8   Death Comes to The Hibiscus – stage play
    The Essential Heart – radio play
    (writing as Nicholas Vane)
9   Send for Paul Temple – stage play
10 The Teckman Biography (tv serial)
11 Paul Temple and Steve (radio serial)
12 Twenty Minutes From Rome – a teleplay
13 Portrait of Alison – tv serial
14 Paul Temple: Two Plays for Radio Volume 1
15 Three Plays for Radio Volume 2
16 The Other Man – tv serial
17 Paul Temple and the Spencer Affair – radio serial
18 Step In The Dark - film script
19 My Friend Charles – tv serial
20 A Case For Paul Temple – radio serial
21 Murder In The Media – more rediscovered serials and
    stories
22 The Desperate People – tv serial
23 Paul Temple: Two Plays For Television
24 And Anthony Sherwood Laughed – radio series
25 The World of Tim Frazer – tv serial
26 Paul Temple Intervenes – radio serial
27 Passport To Danger – radio serial
28 Bat Out of Hell – tv serial
29 Send For Paul Temple Again – radio serial
30 Mr Hartington Died Tomorrow – radio serial

Murder At The Weekend – the rediscovered newspaper serials and short stories

Also published by Williams & Whiting:
Francis Durbridge : The Complete Guide
By Melvyn Barnes

Titles by Francis Durbridge to be published by Williams & Whiting
A Case For Sexton Blake – radio serial
Paul Temple: Two Plays for Radio Volume 2 (contains Send for Paul Temple and News of Paul Temple)
They Knew Too Much – magazine serial

For more information about Francis Durbridge please visit: www.francisdurbridgepresents.com

INTRODUCTION

The entire German-speaking world was in crime fever when a multi-part series based on a script by Francis Durbridge was shown on television. From *Der Andere* (*The Other Man*) (1959) to *Die Kette* (*The Chain*) (1977), the broadcasts of the thrilling cliffhanger stories brought sensational ratings. Often cited as an example is *Das Halstuch* (*The Scarf*) (1961) (still associated today with the inglorious premature betrayal of the culprit by Wolfgang Neuss). However, the 89% audience rating of this multi-part series was topped by the last episode of *Tim Frazer* (1962): 93% viewing was never achieved by a TV programme before or since. Even in 1977, when there were "already" three TV programmes, *The Chain* was the most successful TV programme of the year with almost 72% viewing figures (and also more successful than all the programmes broadcast in 1976).

It is no wonder that the term 'street sweeper', which has since been extended to many other TV events, was invented for Francis Durbridge. The empty streets and pubs, the cinemas, theatres and restaurants without visitors and the postponements of adult education classes and church events when a Durbridge thriller was on TV are well known - not to mention adjourned sessions (even in the Bundestag!).

Of course, other media also wanted to get in on this success. A German theatre producer, for example, managed to buy a play from Durbridge (*Race Against the Clock*), bringing it to the stage almost ten years earlier than in his own country.

Of course, magazines also saw the opportunity to increase their circulation by printing a serialised crime novel by Durbridge.

The master of finely dosed suspense, as the author was often called, was happy to use this opportunity to serve up serialised stories already published in Britain to the German public.

However, since Francis Durbridge was an extraordinary perfectionist and was never content to simply sell something old as new, he used this opportunity to revise these "old stories". Often there were name changes, in one case even the introduction of a new perpetrator.

In the case of *Die Gelbe Windmühle* (*The Yellow Windmill*), a serial that appeared in *Bild und Funk* in the winter of 1965/1966 (issue no. 47/1965 (20.11.1965-26.11.1965)) to issue no. 5/1966 (29.01.1966-04.02.1966)), there is also an English version. Durbridge wrote this for the *Sunday Dispatch* as early as 1954. However, the German version, which appeared eleven years later, has some differences, especially at the beginning.

Bild und Funk gave the publication of Durbridge's eleven-parter a big build-up. With phrases like "Millions of TV sets held their breath! Now also in *BILD UND FUNK* the gripping crime novel by Francis Durbridge" it promoted the crime novel effectively.

At the same time, readers could look forward to an unprecedented competition with countless great prizes.

Readers were invited to participate with the following campaign:
Who kidnapped Susan Kelford?
Play detective! Take part!
Get to the bottom of Durbridge's new crime serial, *The Yellow Windmill*.
Tell your neighbour too
- Tell everyone:
It pays to find the kidnapper!

The successful detectives who guessed the right solution could win valuable prizes such as 20 TV sets, 25 radios, 30 record players, 100 valuable illustrated books and 750 records with Freddy Quinn songs. The total value of the prizes added up to over 40,000 D-marks.

To make the serial visually attractive, some scenes from it were also drawn. At the beginning of each episode, there was a detailed summary listing the suspects, their motives and their behaviour.

After three episodes, the magazine published photos of eager Durbridge detectives giving their opinions on who the culprit was. Entire companies were trying to track down the murderer and kidnapper.

The *Bild und Funk* now ran the headline: "Sensational *BILD UND FUNK* success! Durbridge fever everywhere" and went on to write: "In companies, on the streets, at the bakery, on the train - everywhere Durbridge is once again the talk of the town. The new serial *The Yellow Windmill* is being hotly discussed. There have never been so many amateur detectives! [...] High-tension dramatist Durbridge confuses his readers. Yet more than a few believe they have already figured him out. [...] Durbridge has once again managed to keep people on tenterhooks. Only with one difference: in the television thriller, the streets were deserted. In our serial, the squares fill with discussing detectives."

It was only after the sixth instalment that eager readers were given an address to which they could send a simple postcard with the name of the culprit. The closing date for entries was midnight on 31 December 1965 (the postmark applied).

The Yellow Windmill was published only once as a serial story and this edition is the first time it has appeared in the English market as a complete book. Durbridge fans will be delighted, because the novel offers everything that lovers of the British author like: countless twists and turns, a mysterious object, many suspects, typical surprises and, of course, breathtaking cliffhangers! Exciting entertainment while reading this completely unjustly forgotten Durbridge jewel that has disappeared into oblivion!

Dr Georg Pagitz, January 2021

The Yellow Windmill
Chapter One

There was the child. "Stop there!" The driver obeyed. The man next to him had rolled down the window. He looked across the lawn into the park. All he could see was the little red coat and the chestnut-brown hair above it, and the little hand hurrying after a black poodle that held still, wagging its tail, to be scratched. That had to be her. Susan. He knew Mary Smith's habits well. At this time of day she always sat on a bench at the entrance to Regent's Park and let Susan play on the grass. He pulled his hat deeper into his forehead before opening the door of the limousine and getting out. No one who was not very close to him would recognise him. He quickly glanced left and right. This part of the park was almost empty. No one around except those he was looking for. The mild sun of this autumn day had sunk behind the rooftops; in a few minutes it would begin to darken. He had to hurry. But he walked slowly as he strode towards the little girl. The left hand he held behind his back. The hand with the windmill.

It was indeed a windmill. Carved from wood, about twelve inches high and painted yellow. This was solid work indeed. Its wings turned when you tapped them lightly or blew against them. Just the right tool for the purpose for which he had chosen it. The leaves rustled under his shoes.

The child heard it and turned to him. He didn't flinch. Guilelessly she looked at him, questioning, wide-eyed.

He produced a smile, bent down and pointed to the dog. "Is this yours, Susan?"

The little girl shook her head and let go of the poodle. The man crouched down and pulled his hand out from behind his back. "Look what I have for you..."

Mary Smith sat on the bench reading a letter from her brother. He hadn't been heard from for a long time and now told her how pleased he was that she had been given such a good position in Sir Cedric Kelford's house. The recognition, though belated, filled her with pride. A year ago, after the death of his wife, the bank president had engaged her to look after his young daughter. Susan was now four, a cute child, trusting and quick to learn.

She heard the little girl calling and lowered the letter.

Susan came running towards her. "Look!" She held a yellow windmill aloft above her with both hands, the blades spinning.

Mary Smith smiled and nodded. It often happened that the little girl received gifts from the many people who happened to be passing by in the park. This one seemed to delight her especially.

"I'm so warm," said the little girl, setting down the windmill and beginning to take off her little coat.

"But it's chilly already," Mary protested. "You'll catch cold!"

Susan didn't listen to her. She threw the coat on the bench and took the windmill. Mary sank her eyes back into the letter, and Susan ran off, across the lawn, to the car parked at the side of the road. The man was standing in front of it. He looked around quickly in all directions, then called out to Susan. She ran over to him. The driver had opened the door and folded the back of the passenger seat forward. Quick as a flash, the man grabbed the child and yanked her up. The windmill escaped from her hand and fell to the ground. Susan bristled. Before she could begin to scream, the man threw her into the back seat, his left hand hastily going into his pocket, pulling something out.

Susan's scream was stifled under the chloroformed cloth he pressed over her face. He quickly picked up the yellow windmill, got into the car and pulled the door shut. A moment later the car was gone.

***

The door was yanked open and a man rushed in. Mike Houston recognised him immediately. He had seen his picture countless times in the society columns of London newspapers: it was Sir Cedric Kelford.

Now Kelford's face was pale and looked haggard.

"How could such a thing happen in the middle of London, Inspector..." he groaned.

Houston had risen from behind his desk and bowed. He gestured towards the visitor's desk.

"I can't sit down now, Inspector.... I'm sorry, I didn't quite catch your name on the phone earlier," Kelford said, still agitated but already struggling to regain his usual dignified demeanour.

"Houston," said the Inspector. "Thank you for coming to Scotland Yard so quickly. I thought it best to ask you here so as not to lose any time. Your nanny was wise enough to contact us at once."

"Mary! Where is she?"

"In the next room," Houston said quietly. "A colleague of mine Inspector Loman and I questioned her for almost an hour. Unfortunately without much useful result, I'm afraid."

"But she must have noticed something!" exclaimed Kelford. "She always took such good care of Susan..." His voice failed him. He ran splayed fingers through his dark hair, which was already beginning to turn grey at the temples.

"Wouldn't you rather sit down, sir?" the Inspector asked. Kelford nodded and sank into the chair in front of the desk. He buried his face in his hands.

Houston remained silent.

3

When Kelford raised his head again, his features showed an artificial, stony calm. Only his jaw muscles ground, indicating how aroused he still was. His eyes shone moistly.

"I'm sorry, Inspector," he said, "for letting myself go like that. But Susan" – he swallowed – "is my only child. All I have left since my wife..."

Houston nodded. "I know," he said. "And you can count on it, we'll do everything we can to find her as quickly as possible. A lot of our people are out searching the park right now. I don't know if anything will come of it. But that's where it happened. That's where we have to start looking."

"Yes – yes," Kelford said. "But I just can't get it into my head that Mary didn't see anything, nothing at all. I mean..."

Houston shrugged. "You can ask her yourself!" He reached for the phone and said a few words into it.

Two minutes later Mary Smith was standing in the doorway.

When she saw Kelford, her eyes widened. Then she hung her head and began to sob unrestrainedly.

The man who had been standing behind her in the corridor gently pushed her into the room, entered and closed the door.

"This is Inspector Loman, sir," Houston introduced him. His words were lost in Mary's weeping.

"Do calm down, Mary!" said Kelford. "I don't blame you, for anything. Though I must say that you..." He interrupted himself. "Oh, what's the point of all this?"

He pulled a white handkerchief from his breast pocket and held it out to her. She took it without lifting her eyes, ran it over her eyes and crumpled it between her fingers.

"We've already asked you everything we can think of, Miss Smith," Houston said after everyone had sat down. "But perhaps you should tell Sir Cedric again."

Mary continued haltingly, interrupted again and again by sobs. "My God," she finally said quietly. "The poor child!

4

When I think how amused she was when she came running up to me and showed me that little yellow windmill..."

Houston raised his head and glanced at Loman, who looked at Mary in surprise. "What windmill, Miss Smith? You haven't told us about that before!"

"I must have forgotten in the excitement." There wasn't much she could report.

"A yellow windmill," murmured Inspector Houston thoughtfully. "Can you make anything of that, Sir Cedric?"

Kelford shook his head.

"I think we may assume that the windmill was the means by which the person who abducted Susan lured the child to him," said Inspector Loman. "But I don't see how that can get us anywhere."

Sir Cedric Kelford stood up.

"Come on, Mary!" His voice was feeble. "We're going home."

"Just a moment, sir," Houston said, before Kelford left the room behind Mary Smith. "Do you have any enemies?"

Kelford raised an eyebrow. "Of course I do! Show me the successful man who hasn't enemies! Businesswise, I mean. But one who would do something like this to me – no."

Houston closed the door behind him and turned to his colleague who had stayed behind in the room. "Quite the mysterious business, Loman. Don't you think?"

Loman regarded Houston with a tilted head, as if seeing him properly for the first time. The hard face beneath the dark hair, already streaked with grey. The narrow little beard, the pronounced chin. It was a good, confidence-inspiring face. Only in the eyes, Loman thought, there was sometimes, as now, an expression that didn't suit his face. Loman called him romantic.

"You're forty-seven, Mike, and you've been in this game a long time. You know how it all works. You know the chain of crime'll never end, and we're back to square one every day. What we have to use is our little bit of brains and our experience and, when it comes down to it, our bones. I don't know what drove you to become a detective. For me, it's a job, as good or as bad as any other. For me, there are no mysterious cases. Only solved and unsolved, and even for those there is ultimately a natural explanation. Two and two is still four."

"Listen, Loman," Mike Houston said. "You need to get a different way of looking at things. When are you going to realise that criminals are always trying to make five?"

Loman looked at him, puzzled. "Come on, Mike," he finally said. "Get your coat. We need to see if our people have found anything in Regent's Park."

***

Chief Superintendent Gerald Elder leaned back in his armchair and glanced out of the window of his office at Scotland Yard. "Three days have now passed since the abduction of Susan Kelford," he said. There was no reproach in his tone as he asked the question, "And you've followed up all the leads?"

"Some clues would be good," Inspector Houston replied. "If we had any, we'd be more comfortable." He drew with his ballpoint on the top sheet of his note pad.

"And you didn't get anything more out of the nanny either?"

Houston's colleague Loman took over the answer. "The poor thing is still close to a nervous breakdown now. Sir Cedric Kelford has been damn decent to her. He even tried to comfort her. I'd have whispered something else to her, the silly goose. What was she there for if not to look after the kid!"

Elder didn't respond to Loman's criticism. "Are you sure," he turned to Houston, "that Kelford hasn't received a ransom letter by now, or something of that sort?"

"He hasn't mentioned anything about one, sir."

"I suppose such a letter would have come in the post," said the Superintendent thoughtfully. "The trouble is – Kelford has quite a number of addresses, as you know. After all, he's not only a bank president, he's also a director of several companies."

Houston nodded. "And even if a kidnapper should have made contact with him – it will certainly be a great temptation for Kelford to pay the sum demanded and not tell us anything about it. For fear our intervention might endanger his child."

"Well, in that case he wouldn't be calling on the Deputy Chief of Scotland Yard twice a day, as he does," Loman objected. "Sir Cedric's a great man. He has first-class connections in the highest of places. I have a feeling that if we don't come up with some results soon, he may become quite uncomfortable."

Mike Houston raised his hands and dropped them again. "But I don't see what else we can do. We've had Regent's Park and the canal dragged – result nothing. We've questioned everyone who lives near where it happened – again nothing. We've checked every scoundrel who has ever been involved in a kidnapping affair – still nothing. Television and radio have twice carried search reports, the press is helping us – and yet nothing. Not the slightest trace. The child ran into the park and disappeared. That's all we know. No point to start from. It's so maddening!"

He shrugged his shoulders. "Could it have been one of those women with psychological problems who steal little children because they feel so lonely and suffer from unfulfilled maternal longings? That would at least explain why there was no ransom letter. But even in that case..."

"There've been cases like this before. But..." sighed Superintendent Elder, "we've nothing positive to report if Kelford calls again." He began to blow on his pipe. Houston and Loman saw that he was squeezing the tobacco far too tightly. They knew this sign. Their boss was displeased and angry without betraying it by saying a word.

"I feel sorry for Kelford too," Houston began again. "That's the reason I'm working on this case day and night. I've put myself in his shoes. When I think of how I would have felt if something like this had happened to one of my children when they were that age..." He clenched his fists.

"How are both of yours, by the way?" asked Superintendent Elder, trying to distract and reassure his colleague.

Houston's face brightened. He was a widower and a rather secretive one at that. On duty, he hardly said anything about his private life. But when asked about his son and daughter....
"Dennis is doing well in his job. You know, he works at the Central Bank."

"Isn't that the bank whose president is Sir Cedric Kelford..." Immediately, the Superintendent's mind flashed back to the case they had to solve.

Houston confirmed it.

"And your daughter?" inquired Elder further. "Didn't she want to go into the theatre?"

"Yes, and she's making her way there, too," Houston said proudly. "Look!" He reached into his breast pocket, pulled out a newspaper clipping and handed it over to Elder.

"Only twenty-two and already starring in a television play," Elder read aloud. "She certainly has done well for herself," he added.

"It's going to be shown on Sunday," Houston said.

"I'll make a point of watching it," his superior announced. "That reminds me – didn't I read somewhere that she's supposed to be engaged to the playwright?"

"That's a bit of an exaggeration. You shouldn't believe everything you read in the press." Houston hastily defended. "Although they are good friends."

Elder smiled. "I can tell you don't like this chap Knight much, do you? Wants to rob you of your only daughter, does he..."

Houston tried to smile too. He didn't quite succeed. "I've nothing against him. He seems to be quite a capable fellow at his trade."

"Well, we'll see for ourselves on Sunday, won't we, Loman?"

"I'm looking forward to it too, sir," Loman declared.

"So, gentlemen," Elder became serious again, "now let's comb through all the reports from our people on the Susan Kelford case together. We may yet find a tiny clue."

The three men worked in silence. Suddenly there was a knock at the door and a uniformed sergeant entered. "Package for Inspector Houston, sir," he reported. "Received by special courier just now."

As the officer left the room, Houston looked at the small package. It was tied with string. The sender had addressed it in block letters to Houston personally. He opened it.

Out of the wrapping paper came a cardboard box. On the lid was a small note.

Houston skimmed the scribbled pencil writing. "Listen!" he said excitedly and read out: "I can give you a tip in the Kelford case. You'll see from what this packet contains that I know what I am talking about. Meet me at 'Skipper's Haunt' in Chatham on Sunday at seven o'clock in the evening." The letter was signed 'Nobbler Williams'.

Houston tossed the note aside and tore open the box. The three men stared inside.

"Why, it's..."

It was a little yellow windmill.

***

A little yellow windmill. A pretty toy. And yet – it had served an unscrupulous criminal to lure and kidnap a child. Mike Houston and the two others had examined the windmill thoroughly but found no further clues.

Houston put it back on the desk. "Nobbler Williams," he muttered.

"What are we coming to when men like that are signing the nicknames they go by in the underworld," Superintendent Elder growled.

"Yeah," Houston said. "Nobbler – the 'pug'. A petty thief of opportunity. Every now and then he gets involved in something bigger. I know him. He got involved in a bank robbery in Hammersmith once. Got two months for his part in it then got early release for good behaviour. I haven't heard anything adverse about him since. I think he's working on some coastal steamer now as a coal trimmer."

"That would explain why he wants you to meet him at Chatham," Elder said.

"Should we inform our colleagues in Chatham beforehand?" Houston asked.

Elder shook his head. "No. Take matters into your own hands! We can still communicate with our colleagues there later if necessary."

"All right, sir. But I'll take Loman with me. Just in case."

Houston reached for the windmill.

"Right now, though, I'm going to take another look at that nanny."

***

That evening, Inspector Mike Houston didn't get home until after nine o'clock. Nevertheless, his son Dennis greeted him with the exclamation, "You're home already, Dad?"

Houston knew it wasn't meant ironically. Since the Susan Kelford case had been on his mind, he had been on the road almost constantly. For the last few nights he hadn't slept for more than five hours.

Mary Smith had burst into tears again at the sight of the yellow windmill. That had remained the only result of his visit. Nevertheless, the feeling that all his efforts were futile had left him. The meeting with Nobbler Williams would bring him closer to solving the case. He felt sure of it.

Silently, he took off his hat and coat and went into the living room. Dennis put down the magazine he had been reading. "How about the Kelford case, Dad? Anything new to report?"

Mike Houston reached for his pipe and filled it. "You know I don't talk out of school as a matter of principle." He pushed the mouthpiece between his teeth.

"But it's been days since that poor kid was taken. The police must be doing something!"

"We certainly are doing something!" retorted Houston sharply. "That at least I can say."

"I'm sorry, Dad. I didn't mean it that way, you know that. But you must understand – the little girl is, after all, the daughter of my most senior boss."

"That's all right, Dennis. I know," Houston grumbled. "But we don't want to discuss police business here. It's not like I'm asking you about your clients' banking secrets."

Silently, Dennis reached for his magazine again. Houston exhaled dark clouds of smoke and looked at his son. Wavy dark hair, a narrow smooth face that seemed somehow unfinished. The vivid brown eyes that always reminded Houston of his late wife. The boy has a way about him lately

11

that I don't like, Houston thought. But he's still young, only twenty-four. But what do I actually know about him – really? That he is my son, yes. But other than that...

It wasn't the first time that Mike Houston had pondered about his children and his relationship with them. His job left him little time to look after them. Too little. He knew it, and this knowledge filled him with a certain sense of guilt. But what can I do about it, he thought. This job just eats me up.

He heard the flat door and raised his head. Rona stepped into the room. She pulled the cap off her head and shook her blonde hair, bent down to him and kissed him on the ear. Her cheeks were flushed from the fresh air.

Mike Houston eyed her proudly. "You look rather spiffy in your new outfit."

Rona laughed. "Thanks a lot, Dad. You don't normally notice what I'm wearing."

Houston threatened her with the pipe stem. His good humour was restored. Rona ran out to comb her hair, came back in and dropped into an armchair.

"I've had ten solid hours of rehearsal today! Nothing but rehearsals! Over and over again! Carl is driving us all crazy with his constant changes to the script. If he keeps re-writing the lines like this, it'll be a completely different play before we get on air."

"Well," Dennis said pointedly serious, "you're the one who wanted to be an actress so badly..."

Rona glanced quickly at her father and smiled. Mike Houston had tried for a long time to talk his daughter out of her acting ambitions. She had prevailed. Now that she had succeeded, no one was prouder of her than he was.

"So how's it all coming along?" enquired Dennis. "Is Carl actually rewriting the play during rehearsals?"

Rona shook her head. "Then it would still be possible. Anyway, it wouldn't be so time-consuming. But no, he insists

12

on making the changes only in his flat. He can't work in any other atmosphere he says, the great master. He has to be alone while doing it, he claims."

"Now don't you worry about it," said Mike Houston. "The better the play, the better for you. After all, millions of people will be turning on their television sets on Sunday night to watch it."

"Don't remind me! Millions, yes. Millions of people who notice the slightest mistake." Rona shook herself.

Houston patted her on the shoulder. "Don't get stage fright! You'll do a good job, I'm sure of it!"

Dennis left the room. "I have to cram a bit for my continuing education course." Houston waited until his son had closed the door behind him.

"Tell me, Rona – what's the deal between you and Carl Knight, I mean, are you two as good as engaged?"

Rona hesitated for a moment.

"Don't you like Carl, Dad?"

Houston frowned. "I – I find him a little theatrical."

Rona laughed. "But then, we theatricals all are! Or at least that's how the rest of us appear."

"You haven't answered my question, Rona."

She held out her left hand to him. She wasn't wearing a ring.

"Satisfied?"

"You know as well as I do that a ring doesn't matter," Houston said seriously. "I think you understand where I'm coming from."

"How you police always think the worst!" She smiled again. "But if it makes you feel any better, Dad, we're far too busy with the play to have time or sense for anything else."

She laid her head against his shoulder. "Won't you come to the studio with me on Sunday evening, Dad, and watch the show there? It would help to calm my nerves to have you near me."

He took her hand and stroked it.

"I would so love to come, love. You know that. But I'm busy. Especially on Sunday night."

***

Mike Houston had decided to consult his colleagues in Chatham after all. He and Inspector Loman had already arrived in the harbour town, twenty-five miles east of London, in the afternoon. But the only thing the Chatham detectives could do for the two Scotland Yard detectives was to show them the way to the pub Nobbler Williams had indicated as the meeting place: 'The Skipper's Haunt'.

It was a small, sparse pub with worn furniture and the usual sailing ship in the bottle above the bar. The crowd seemed to be mostly sailors, talking loudly to each other and still having a drink. A harmless sailor's pub, like countless others in England, Houston thought after looking around.

He and Loman ordered beer and stood at the bar near the window. They talked about the television play Rona was to appear in that evening whilst looking out into the street.

The clock in the back of the room struck seven. "He should be here soon," whispered Loman.

"There he is now," Houston said quietly, nudging him lightly with his elbow.

Across the street, a man walked slowly. The two detectives couldn't see his face clearly. But Houston had recognised Nobbler Williams immediately. Every idiosyncrasy of one of his "clients" was indelibly imprinted on Houston's mind.

Nobbler Williams was wearing, as always, a coat that was two sizes too big and hung limply down his figure. His hat was on at an angle and the brim was bent down low over his right eye.

14

He walked with his hands buried deep in his pockets, obviously lost in thought.

"I think he's going past..." Houston hissed in surprise.

In fact, Nobbler Williams was traipsing along the opposite pavement twenty yards away, almost out of sight of the two detectives.

Suddenly he veered towards the roadway to cross it.

That's when Houston saw the car. When Williams took the first step onto the road, the big American limousine was still twenty yards away. But then it accelerated and sped off.

Williams jumped off the road back towards the pavement.

Houston saw the driver jerk the wheel around. The car shot towards Williams....

A scream pierced thinly into the pub. An engine howled. Houston and Loman rushed out, ran across the street, towards the dark bundle lying lifeless in the gutter.

The car was gone. A crowd of curious people quickly gathered around the spot where the man who had once been Nobbler Williams was lying.

Houston knelt down. "There's nothing you can do about it now, Loman..."

Someone tapped Houston on the shoulder. As he straightened up, he saw a uniformed policeman. Houston rose fully and took him aside. "I'm Inspector Houston from Scotland Yard," he said.

"I have the number of the car, sir," the policeman reported, handing him a piece of paper. "As it happens, I was just patrolling along here when..."

"Good," Houston said. "Call the station and order an ambulance. More correct maybe that would be a hearse."

**

Loman got behind the wheel as they drove back to London. Houston was silent, staring at the road.

"Damn," he expressed after a long time. "That this had to happen, in front of us. Now that we finally had a viable lead, and then.... This hit-and-run is the best proof that Nobbler Williams really knew something important about the Kelford case. I feel sorry for him, by the way. He was a crook all right, but one of the amusing ones. Oh!" He clenched his fist in annoyance and slapped his knee with it.

"Did you recognise anything about the fellow who was driving the car?" asked Loman.

"Not much," growled Houston. "It was too dark! He was wearing a scarf and had his hat pulled low over his face. That's all."

He snorted. "In this case, everything's gone wrong so far. Drop me off at Putney, Loman. I'll take the bus from there. I should be able to make it home before my daughter gets back from the TV studio. At least something good's happened today."

"All right," Loman said. "Give me the slip of paper with the car registration number. I'll see what we can find out about it back at the Yard. If there is anything, I'll call you at home."

Houston sank back into silence. The way the man at the wheel had put on his hat, the scarf....

He tried to recall the image. It reminded him of someone. But who? When he thought of Rona, it came to him.

The young man his daughter had brought home a couple of times in the last week – Carl Knight!

Houston immediately dismissed the thought. It was absurd. What on earth would Carl Knight have been doing in Chatham tonight? Of all nights, the night when his play was being broadcast on television! Surely Knight wouldn't miss watching the broadcast of his own television play.

I'm overworked, Houston thought. That's what this is all about. That's how you get the craziest ideas.

16

He was nervous. And dissatisfied. More dissatisfied than ever.

***

As she removed her make-up and the tension of the last hour and a half slowly faded from her, Rona Houston felt happy. She had succeeded, she knew that. The play had been received with great applause by the audience. The many enthusiastic calls even during the broadcast proved it. Too bad, that picture glitch shortly after the start of the transmission. The director was almost in despair when he received the message. But the audience had put up with it and continued to watch. And that was the main thing. Millions had seen her, Rona Houston, play her first leading role!

Mavis Long, a colleague, looked in at the door. "Goodbye, Rona! You were great, darling!"

"Thanks. But tell me – do you have any idea where Carl is?"

"No, Rona. I haven't seen him all evening. It's possible he was here and left when the technical glitch happened right at the beginning. Maybe it was too much for his frail nerves!"

She disappeared.

As Rona left the studio, she met Terry Smith, the director. "Any word from Carl?" he asked.

She shook her head.

"I've no idea where he got to. I can only think he took himself home to watch it from there. He could at least have called afterwards to congratulate us all. Goodness, it's raining again. Come under my umbrella, Rona, I'll walk you to the bus."

"Thanks, Terry, but I'll take a taxi." She asked at the porter's lodge if Carl might have called in the meantime, but the porter replied in the negative.

17

"Crap weather," growled the taxi driver who drove her to Carl Knight's flat. "It's been pouring non-stop. Has been for hours. So, here we are. Do you live here, or should I wait?"

"No, thanks. You go ahead."

Rona rang the bell at Carl Knight's flat. But no one answered. She was about to turn back when she saw the hall light come on. A moment later, the door opened.

Carl stood before her in a dark green dressing gown. His black hair was dishevelled and he looked pale. "Ah, it's you, Rona..." he said nervously.

"Were you expecting someone else?"

"No, no – not that I know of." He hesitated for a moment, then said, "But do come in, darling!"

She followed him into the living room.

"Carl, you're not... I mean, you did like the play. Didn't you?"

His facial muscles suddenly tensed. "The play? Yes, yes. Of course I did. The performance was great. You were wonderful!"

"And, you mean that the beginning..."

"Excellent!" he interrupted her. "Quite excellent!"

A suspicion assailed her. All of a sudden. Carl hadn't seen the programme at all! It couldn't be otherwise. Not to mention that he obviously knew nothing about the technical incident at the beginning of the show – he also said nothing about the acting performances in detail.

Rona was confused. For weeks they had been discussing this play over and over again, talking their heads off. And now... It had never occurred to her that anything in the world could be more important to Carl Knight on this Sunday evening than watching the broadcast of his play.

Carl broke the awkward silence. "Drink, darling?"

She avoided his gaze. "No, thanks. I'm tired. It's been very tiring. I want to go home."

18

Carl Knight nodded and grabbed her arm. He hesitated for a moment, as if he wanted to say something. But then he lowered his hand and escorted Rona to the door.

On her way through the long hallway, Rona's hand brushed something damp. It was Carl's mackintosh.

***

Ever since Loman had dropped him off at a bus stop in Putney, Mike Houston had been thinking incessantly about Nobbler Williams' death. He had tried to put the thought out of his mind, at least for this evening, when his daughter Rona would surely return home beaming with joy. But the murder at Chatham was on his mind.

What would Sir Cedric Kelford say if he learned that the only lead to his abducted child no longer existed?

Did he do something wrong? Houston asked himself. But what should he have done?

An instinct born of his long police experience told him that there was far more to this affair than just the kidnapping of a little girl.

So far, Kelford had still not received a ransom letter. But what was the purpose of the kidnapper if he didn't intend to extort a large ransom from the banker?

Houston couldn't shake the feeling that more was about to happen. That Susan's abduction was only the first blow against Kelford. Perhaps something else would happen soon.

He slid the flat key into the lock and opened the door. It was dark inside. It was only eleven and Rona wouldn't be able to get back here for at least half an hour.

As he was about to push the hall door shut, he heard the sound of a car from outside, then Rona's voice.

He waited. Rona came up the stairs. "You're here sooner than I thought," he called out to her. "Well, how did it go?"

"The performance was very good," she said softly.

19

"Is something the matter? Has something happened? Oh, silly me, come in first!"

He went ahead into the living room and pressed the switch next to the door. A light came on.

"Well, Dennis..."

An armchair stood four yards from the television, with its back to the door. The screen flickered white.

Dennis seemed to have fallen asleep during the broadcast. His right arm hung over the arm of the chair, his head was slumped on his shoulder.

Mike Houston reached out to wake him up.

He took a step closer. Then froze.

"What..."

He wheeled around. "Call the doctor, Rona, quick, quick!" His voice was low and raspy. Rona barely understood him.

"What is it, Dad? Is he ill?"

"He's been shot! Quick, quick, phone the doctor!"

Rona rushed to the phone. Inspector Mike Houston bent lower over his son. And immediately he knew: it was too late. With dragging steps, as if stunned, Houston went to the television set to turn it off. He heard Rona speaking excitedly on the phone.

His finger on the off button, he bristled as his gaze caught sight of something.

Close above the screen, carved into the wood, was a small drawing. In yellow pen. It was of a yellow windmill.

Chapter Two

Mike Houston stood with his back to the body. He lowered his finger from the television's off button and stared at the small drawing in the wood border above the screen.

It was a crude sketch. Quickly scratched in with a yellow pen, the killer had had no time to lose. But there was no doubt what it was supposed to represent. A windmill. A yellow windmill.

Houston wheeled around as he heard words behind him. He glanced at the door. Rona was holding onto the door knob with one hand, as if she needed a prop. Her face was white.

"What did you say?" he asked harshly.

"The doctor's not answering." Slowly, with unsteady steps, she came into the room. Startled, she glanced towards the armchair and immediately turned her head away. Suddenly tears welled up in her eyes and ran down her cheeks. "My God," she choked out. "Dennis... Is he really..."

"Yes." Houston stepped up beside her and put his left arm around her shoulders. He was breathing heavily and audibly. "He's dead."

Rona turned her head once more to face her dead brother. She saw the bullet hole, her face contorted. Houston gently pulled her back and pushed her aside.

"This is no place for you, Rona." His voice sounded toneless. "Call the hospital, have them send an ambulance. And then go to bed. You're going to need all the strength you can muster."

"But I can't sleep now, Dad. I..."

"At least try! There's nothing you can do here."

She nodded silently and went out.

Inspector Houston began to examine the room methodically. He heard the buzz of the dial from the hallway.

21

Rona's tear-strangled voice, the murmur as the receiver clicked into the fork, Rona's footsteps moving away.

He found the bullet that had pierced his son's head. It was lodged in the upholstery of the armchair. It had obviously been fired from the direction of the television.

Only now did Houston notice that the screen was still shimmering white. He switched the set off and dropped into an armchair.

Hopefully the ambulance would come soon. Houston was alone with his dead son. He couldn't remember ever feeling so helpless.

Dennis... Murdered! Who could have done this? For what reason could Dennis have been murdered – a young, harmless, conscientious bank employee?

And what did the drawing of the yellow windmill on the television set mean?

Was there any connection between Dennis Houston and the kidnapping of Sir Cedric Kelford's young daughter?

The shrill ring of the telephone jolted him out of his thoughts and, half stunned, he dragged himself into the hallway and picked up the phone. He muttered his name.

"Is that you, Mike?" asked the familiar voice of his colleague Loman.

"Yes, what is it?"

"The people from Chatham just called. They want us to attend the post-mortem of Nobbler Williams. Tomorrow morning at..."

"I'm sorry, Loman," Houston said quietly, "but you'll have to go." He gave a terse account of what had happened.

"But that's..." Loman fell silent. Houston didn't say a word either.

It was a long time before Loman began to speak again. "Mike, I... I don't think I need to tell you how I feel about..."

"It's all right, Loman," Houston interrupted him. "I know, and I thank you. But you must understand – I still can't believe it."

Loman let another minute pass. "Have you found any leads, Mike?"

He began to ask a series of questions that Houston had already put to himself. But there was no explanation, no clue to the perpetrator. Not yet.

"I can hear a car coming, Loman. That'll be the ambulance from the hospital. I've got to hang up."

"Just one more thing, Mike. I ran the number of the car that Nobbler Williams was run over with. The number plate was bogus."

"I'm not surprised," Houston said. His voice was calm now. He hung up the phone and opened the door for the ambulance men.

***

The next twenty-four hours always seemed surreal to Mike Houston when he recalled them later.

He hadn't been able to sleep that night. He vaguely kept in mind that there had been a conference at Scotland Yard that morning. There'd been condolences from colleagues and superiors. In the early afternoon came the coroner's inquest, at which he identified his son, in accordance with regulations, and described the discovery of the body. The coroner had concluded the short official act by saying: "Murder committed by a person or persons unknown."

It was not until mid-afternoon, as Houston sat facing his daughter in the living room, that his thoughts gradually began to clear.

"What's going to happen now?" asked Rona as she poured him his second cup of tea.

"The matter will take its usual course," he said. "The Assistant Commissioner has offered to assign the case to someone else. That's very considerate of him. But I made it clear that I'll not rest until I myself have found out who murdered Dennis. The main thing is to proceed normally. Whoever did it – we must not arouse suspicion to the murderer that we are on our guard. You too, Rona, must behave, as far as possible, as you normally would."

Rona looked at him questioningly. "You know that on Thursday evening our play is to be performed again, Dad. Do you think I should still go on and do it again in spite of what the papers have said?"

He nodded. "If you feel up to it, yes."

"Of course," Rona said, "though it won't be easy for me." She looked up. "I think that was the doorbell."

"You just sit tight, I'll go and check." Houston went to the flat door and opened it.

"Sir Cedric!" he called out in surprise.

"May I come in, Inspector?"

Houston took his hat and coat from him and escorted the bank president into the living room. When he caught sight of Rona, Sir Cedric Kelford paused in his steps for a moment before continuing towards her.

He was obviously very impressed by her appearance. Houston introduced them to each other. Kelford bowed to her before settling into an armchair.

"I apologise for just barging in here like this, Miss Houston, but..." he turned to the inspector, "the Assistant Commissioner told me what happened here." Kelford bowed his head. "He also told me," he continued after a pause, "that he advised you to withdraw from the case." He looked at Houston inquiringly. "I hope you won't do that, Inspector."

"Do you have any particular reason for that wish, Sir Cedric?" asked Mike Houston. Kelford's tone had also sounded urgent. Had something else happened?

Sir Cedric Kelford leaned forward. "I am convinced that your son's death is in some way connected to my daughter's abduction," he said forcefully. "And the link between the two cases is the yellow windmill."

"It looks that way," Houston replied calmly.

"I'm sure you're the best man to solve this mystery!" exclaimed Kelford. "Besides, I realise that this matter means more to you than just a routine case."

"You can be sure of that," Houston assured him grimly. "But I'm sorry to tell you that we're still as much in the dark as ever."

"You have no explanation of what the drawing of the yellow windmill on your television set might mean?"

Houston shook his head. "For hours I've lain awake coming up with dozens of theories. Yet none make any sense whatsoever." He heaved a deep sigh.

Kelford nervously drummed the fingers of his right hand on his right knee. "If there's anything I can do to help you, let me know."

"There is already something you could do for me," Houston said slowly. "I would appreciate it if you would use your influence as president of the bank to have some discreet investigations made into Dennis."

Kelford nodded. "Of course. But I can tell you right now that you won't learn anything about your son that you don't already know. I had his personnel file sent to me this morning. And you know, we bankers check our employees very carefully. I didn't find anything that wasn't normal."

Houston shrugged. "I have to admit, I'm surprised myself at how little I know about him. You understand – I'm on the road a lot.... It seems to me that he's led a life like all other young bank employees. He played a bit of tennis, took an evening class to further his education. His only hobby was stamp collecting. There was no girl he was particularly friendly with.... He only had one trusted friend – Bob Harridge, who worked with him in the same department."

Kelford turned to Rona.

"Perhaps Miss Houston knows something more?" he asked politely.

"I'm sorry," Rona replied, "but I'm afraid I don't know any more about Dennis either. We were good friends, Dennis and me. Of course we were. But we never confided anything special to each other."

"You see," Houston said helplessly. "Nothing, nothing at all, that could help us."

"Have you spoken to this Bob Harridge yet, Inspector?"

"Yes. When I told him what happened, he stared at me as if I wasn't in my right mind – he was that upset."

"I will assign two of our best investigators to look into the matter," the bank president explained. "They will interview everyone in our company who knew your son. I will send you the reports."

"I would be very grateful." Houston changed the subject. "And you've heard nothing further about your daughter?"

Kelford shook his head. "Not a word..." He looked at his watch, rose and shook hands with Rona and the Inspector. Before leaving, he complimented Rona on her first appearance on television. "I didn't even know you were the Inspector's daughter until I read it in the paper..."

Rona watched him go as he climbed into his grey Rolls Royce.

The assurance that emanated from Sir Cedric Kelford had impressed her deeply.

***

The next morning Rona Houston was called from the garage in the next street. Her little car had been repaired. Rona picked it up and drove to the television studio where a special rehearsal of her play was scheduled.

As she drove the car through the heavy traffic, she thought about her last encounter with Carl Knight. After everything that has happened since Sunday night, we need to have a good talk, she thought to herself.

But Carl Knight hadn't turned up for the rehearsal. Terry Smith, the director, and her fellow actors offered their condolences to Rona. They didn't ask any questions and were obviously trying to cheer her up a little.

Only Carl... He must have read the reports in the papers like everyone else. But he hadn't even called.

When the tea break started, Rona separated from the others and walked down the street to a nearby small cafeteria. She was deeply depressed.

She put her gloves and the manuscript of the play on a chair at an empty table and stood at the end of the queue in front of the long counter.

When she returned to the table with a cup of tea and a biscuit, a man and a girl were sitting there.

The man immediately jumped at the sight of her.

"Bob Harridge!" exclaimed Rona. "Well, this is a surprise!"

"You can say that again! Rona! I haven't seen you for ages!" He brushed back a recalcitrant lock of hair that had fallen onto his forehead.

Rona had been to the cinema a few times with her brother's friend. But in the last few months she had lost contact with him.

Bob pointed to the girl at the table. "Rona – this is Mary Latimer."

The black-haired girl with the large, heavily made-up mouth and deep-set green eyes held out a neat white hand. "I heard what happened to your brother, Miss Houston. I'm very sorry for you."

Rona couldn't explain what it was, but something about Mary Latimer's manner irritated her.

"Has the bank let you go early today then, Bob?" Rona asked as she sat down.

"I went to HR and had to tell them what I knew about Dennis," Bob Harridge replied. "It wasn't worth going back to work after that."

Rona would have liked to ask him some questions, but the presence of the other girl stopped her. She didn't like Mary Latimer.

She wondered why a man like Bob Harridge was apparently well acquainted with a girl who looked richly exotic in these surroundings. Mary Latimer seemed striking. Strange that she should be to the taste of a proper young bank clerk.

"Mary met Dennis once at a dance," Bob said. "She was beside herself when she heard the news."

Mary Latimer took little part in the conversation. She sat and listened. Every now and then she let a quick glance wander around the room.

Bob Harridge was just telling Rona that he had admired her in the Sunday night television performance when she felt a hand on her shoulder. She spun around and looked up. Standing behind her was Carl Knight.

"I thought I'd find you here," he said quietly.

Rona saw that his facial muscles were tense. Around the eyes he looked as if he had slept badly.

She introduced him to Bob Harridge and Mary Latimer. And she saw a cynical smile flicker very briefly around Mary Latimer's mouth as she shook hands with Carl Knight.

It seemed to Rona for a moment as if they already knew each other. She thought no more about it. She could have been mistaken.

Bob Harridge glanced at his watch. "I'm afraid I have to go. Are you coming, Mary?"

Mary Latimer rose to her feet. Carl Knight and Rona made no attempt to hold her back.

Knight waited until they were out of earshot, then moved closer to Rona. "I went by your house this morning to see you. Your father was there. He told me what happened to Dennis. Of course, I'd already read it in the papers. Your father seems to think it's all connected with the Kelford case. Is that really true, or is your father understandably a bit over the top and seeing connections where there aren't any?"

"Of course not," Rona said. She wondered why Carl seemed so concerned.

She told him how they had found Dennis. "And there was a drawing of a yellow windmill on the television."

Carl Knight listened intently.

When she'd finished her narrative, he didn't ask any more questions. He just lit a cigarette. Rona saw that his hand was shaking as he slipped the cigarette case back into his jacket.

"Would you be good enough to get me another cup of tea, Carl?" she asked him, trying to shoo away the tension. "I think you could do with one too," she added.

A little confused, he obeyed. When he returned to their table a few minutes later with the filled cups and sat down with her again, Rona said, "Well, Carl, I have a few questions for you too..."

Knight frowned. "Go on then," he said.

She took a deep breath before asking him, "Are you quite sure, Carl, that you saw the play on TV on Sunday night?"

"But of course I did!" He raised his hands. "I don't understand what you mean, Rona."

She lowered her eyes and stared into her cup. "I was just a bit surprised that you didn't say anything at all about the technical glitch at the beginning. And when I left, I noticed a wet mackintosh on your coat rack. Were you really not out in the rain that night?"

Carl Knight looked at her. Rona raised her head.

"Of course not, Rona. If you must know, a friend visited me and brought back the coat he'd borrowed from me a week before. Just as the show started, he arrived. It irritated me to bits his being there, of course. But what could I do? He stayed and we watched the play together. That's all."

His voice sounded annoyed.

"It's all right, Carl," Rona said amicably. "I'm sorry, but I really was a bit mixed up that night. And what's happened since..."

Carl Knight stroked her forearm briefly and withdrew his hand again.

He reached for his teacup and drank. He fell silent and averted his eyes from Rona. He seemed to be thinking about something that was very much on his mind.

Finally, Rona broke the silence. "I have to get back to rehearsal, Carl," she said in her old, companionable tone. "Are you coming?"

He stood up at the same time as her. "No, I've things to do." A smile slid across his tired-looking face. "I've changed what needed to be changed. Terry will be quite happy if I don't turn up. Otherwise he'll end up thinking I want to rewrite the whole play."

They said goodbye outside the cafeteria.

***

When Rona arrived at the rehearsal studio, Terry Smith, the director, waved her over. "For what I'm about to rehearse, I don't need you, Rona. Go home, and get some rest!"

Rona tried to smile. "Thanks, Terry. I do think I could use a little rest. Well then – see you tomorrow."

She returned to her car.

Have I actually been fair to Carl? she asked herself as she got behind the wheel. She lowered her hands from the wheel and thought about her relationship with him.

She liked Carl Knight. She couldn't put her finger on what it was about him that attracted her so much. He wasn't handsome, though a good-looking man. He wasn't rich, though already successful. There was no calmness and security emanating from him that could have made a woman feel safe. Rona admitted to herself that at times there was something rather unsettling about Carl. Was it his cleverness that had won her over?

Whatever it was, she liked him, and more than that. Did she love him? She had often tried to answer that question for herself. Always in vain. But the fact that she herself wasn't clear about her feelings for him – did that give her the right to be suspicious of him and to ask him questions? After all, she wasn't engaged to him. His private life was none of her business, she told herself.

Perhaps his visitor on Sunday evening had been a girl? Was that why Carl had been so uncomfortable even that evening, that she, Rona, had turned up at his place so late?

Besides, she knew he was working on the plan for a new play. At this stage he had no sense of anything else and often seemed introverted and barely responsive. Rona shook her head at her own behaviour. She had done Carl an injustice.

Unsatisfied with herself, she started the car and drove off. She turned into Baker Street. Her gaze brushed the entrance to a shopping arcade. First she saw the man. His way of moving his shoulders seemed familiar. He had his back to her and was talking to a girl. As she slowly drove on, she kept an eye on the two of them. And then Rona recognised them. It was Carl Knight and Mary Latimer! They were talking animatedly to each other.

Rona suppressed her first impulse to stop. She continued towards Oxford Street.

So she hadn't been mistaken after all! Carl and Mary Latimer had known each other before they were introduced in the cafeteria.

What's going on? ran through Rona's head. There were always new mysteries and events that left one confused and unsure.

She had to force herself to pay attention to the traffic.

She'd been under the impression that Mary Latimer was going out with Bob Harridge that night. How did she manage to get rid of Bob and meet up with Carl?

Or was their meeting a chance encounter?

Questions upon questions...

Rona was thinking as she drove over the Albert Bridge. Suddenly she saw a truck coming right at her car. The driver seemed to have lost control of his vehicle in the middle of the bridge. The lorry was getting closer. A few more seconds and it would collide with her. Rona acted with lightning speed. She had only one option. She jerked the wheel around and pressed the accelerator.

She felt a hard jolt as her car went over the high curb. Luckily for her, there were no pedestrians on this part of the bridge. The truck shot past her by mere inches. Twenty yards further on, Rona steered her car back onto the roadway. Her hands trembled on the steering wheel. She stopped, turned in her seat and looked back.

She expected the truck to stop too, or maybe crash into the guardrail or something like that. But the truck kept going and disappeared towards Oakley Street.

Rona waited a few minutes to recover from her fright. Only then did she drive on, her mind still on the strange incident. Two miles further on, the thought suddenly flashed through her mind: had the lorry been deliberately driven at her? Had someone tried to ram her car in order to...?

Rona hardly dared to finish this thought. She tried to push the thought away. But it didn't leave her mind until she got home.

She found a note from her father. He asked her to pick him up from Scotland Yard at 8 pm.

Rona went to the kitchen and prepared dinner. Keeping busy with the household chores distracted her a little. The telephone rang, she picked up the receiver and to her surprise recognised the voice of Mary Latimer.

"I must speak to you urgently, Miss Houston," she said hastily. "I have found out something very important about your brother Dennis."

"Don't you think it would be better if you called my father at Scotland Yard?" asked Rona.

"No," insisted Mary Latimer. "I must speak to you first. You'll understand when I explain it to you later."

"But I can't tonight," Rona objected coolly.

"Tomorrow morning then," Mary Latimer urged. "It would be best if we met in the cafeteria."

"All right," Rona said, and hung up.

***

Punctually as arranged, Inspector Mike Houston left the Scotland Yard building. He walked with a slight stoop.

How tired he looks, Rona thought, waiting for him outside her car. He tried a smile as he greeted her. There were deep dark circles around his eyes.

"Before we go home, I have to go to Wimpole Street," Mike Houston said after they got in. He gave the address.

"Anything new, Dad?"

Houston nodded. "We found the car that Nobbler Williams was run over with. It was abandoned in a field near Hertford."

"And who does it belong to? Do you know that already?"

"Yes," said Houston. "A certain Dr Spedro in Wimpole Street."

"That's why you want to go there," Rona observed. "Will it take long? I've already made a start on this evening's supper..."

"Not too long, probably," Houston interrupted her reassuringly. "However, I'll have to ask the doctor a few questions. Of course, there's also the possibility that the car could have been stolen from him."

"I think we're almost there," Rona said after a while. She slowed down and tried to read one of the house numbers.

"It must be about here somewhere. Oops, what's going on?"

Rona stopped. Houston followed her gaze.

An ambulance was parked in front of Dr Spedro's house.

The front door was opened, a short dark-haired man appeared and spoke to two white-clad orderlies who dragged a stretcher out of the house past him.

The driver of the ambulance had got out and opened the rear doors. Carefully, the two porters lifted the stretcher and slowly pushed it into the van. Rona leaned forward.

"But..." was all she could say.

"What is it?" asked Houston sharply. "You don't know the person on the stretcher, do you?"

"Yes," Rona said quietly.

"Well – who is it?"

"It's a girl called Mary Latimer..."

Chapter Three

They leaned back into the upholstery to stay in the dark and peered through the windshield screen. Mike Houston and his daughter Rona. The rear door of the ambulance in front of them was open. Carefully, two porters pushed the stretcher inside.

"What do you know about this Mary Latimer?" asked Houston quickly.

Rona didn't take her eyes off the slender figure on the stretcher. "I just met her this afternoon. She was with Bob Harridge. And when I got home earlier, she called. She claimed she needed to see me urgently. She seemed quite upset and said she had some information about Dennis..."

The little man who had come out of the house earlier was apparently giving final instructions to the orderlies. Then he left them and returned to the house.

Mike Houston waited until the orderlies closed the door of the ambulance, got out and walked over to them.

"Would you mind telling me where you are taking the patient?" he asked.

They looked at him dismissively for a moment. But after Houston had identified himself, the older man said, "I don't see why we shouldn't tell you, sir. We're taking her to a nursing home on Martineau Road."

"Do you happen to know what's wrong with her?"

The man shook his head. "The doctor said something about a heart attack. Or something like that. I really can't say for sure. All I know is that we're supposed to drive extra carefully."

Houston thanked him and turned back to Rona.

"Wait for me here!" Before Rona could answer, he went to the door of the house behind which the little man had disappeared and rang the bell. He heard a buzzing sound and pushed the door open.

To the girl in the white coat who received him, he gave his name. "I would like to see Dr Spedro. On a private matter."

The receptionist disappeared into the next room, reappeared after a few seconds and held the door open for him.

"Dr Spedro will see you now."

Houston had entered many consulting rooms in the course of his long professional life. He noticed immediately that something was different here from the usual. He couldn't have said what triggered this feeling in him.

It was a set-up as found in all medical consulting rooms: a long leather couch, a changing room in the corner, a desk and two large glassed-in cabinets in which instruments flashed and medicine samples were stacked.

But something about it was different...

Houston just didn't know what.

Dr Spedro had risen from behind his desk and pointed to the visitor's chair. He was a smooth Italian type with black hair, pale face and bluish shaved skin. His dark, almost black eyes looked at Mike Houston with interest.

"What can I do for you, Inspector?"

Houston hadn't been mistaken. The doctor spoke with an Italian accent, albeit a faint one now.

"It concerns your car, sir," Houston began.

Spedro raised an eyebrow. "Oh yes," he said briskly. "Did the police finally find it? It's been almost a week since I filed the report."

He leaned back in his chair. His heavy eyelids half dropped, giving his gaze something inscrutable.

Houston immediately felt that he had to take the initiative quickly. Spedro is trying to play the superior man, he thought.

Houston quickly asked a series of questions about the car and its disappearance.

Spedro answered just as quickly. Twice he assured Houston that he had already described everything in detail at the police station. According to his account, the car had been stolen from him outside the home of a medical instrument company in Bloomsbury.

"Hmm." Houston looked sharply at the doctor. "I'm not actually here about this theft report..."

"You're not?" Spedro looked taken aback. "Then why exactly are you here?"

Houston let a little pause occur before answering. "With this car, with your car that is, a man was run over on Sunday night."

"What are you saying?"

Houston nodded. "The man's name was Nobbler Williams. Do you know him?"

Dr Spedro shook his head. "Nobbler Williams? I've never heard of him. What did he look like?"

Houston described him.

"No," Dr Spedro said. "I've never seen him. But – you don't suppose I ran him over, do you?"

"After all, it was your car, Doctor," Houston stated.

"But I've already told you – it was stolen from me. Ask at the police station!"

"Can you tell me where you were on Sunday evening, sir?" asked Houston, unperturbed.

"Of course I can." Spedro's voice sounded irritated. "But is this supposed to be an interrogation, Inspector?"

"For the time being, it's a matter of me wanting some questions answered by you," Houston said coolly.

"All right, then. I was staying with friends in Epping. Would you like me to give you the address?"

Without waiting for an answer, Dr Spedro tore a piece of paper from his prescription pad, scribbled something on it and slid the paper across the table to the Inspector.

They heard a noise at the door. Dr Spedro raised his head. "Yes what is it?" he asked angrily.

"There's a telephone call for you," said the receptionist. "It's private."

"Put it through upstairs, would you?" The girl disappeared. Dr Spedro turned to Houston. "I hope you'll excuse me for a few minutes, Inspector."

He left the room and closed the door behind him. Houston stood up and looked around the room. "What is it about this place that makes the atmosphere so different from other consulting rooms," he wondered. The next moment he knew. On a shelf on the wall were models, of various souvenirs.

There was a model of the Eiffel Tower in Paris. A small replica of the Leaning Tower of Pisa. A tiny Black Forest house. And – a carved yellow windmill.

Houston approached the shelf in surprise and took the model down. Thoughtfully he looked at it, turned it in his hands – a yellow windmill....

He heard the door open. Dr Spedro returned.

"Excuse me, Inspector..." He fell silent in mid-sentence and winced when he saw the windmill in the Inspector's hand. For a few seconds he raised his hands as if to snatch the model from Houston, then lowered them again.

Mike Houston pretended to be absorbed in looking at the windmill. But he watched the doctor from the corner of his eye. By the time he turned his full attention to Dr Spedro, the doctor had gone back into self-control mode.

"Do you like it?" asked Spedro in a deliberately harmless tone. "It's a memento – like the other things here." He pointed to the shelf.

"Where did you get it?" asked Houston.

"I brought it back from a trip to Amsterdam once, Inspector," said Spedro. He took the windmill from Houston's hand and put it back in its place. "Yes, what I wanted to say, Inspector – sorry about the interruption, but it was really urgent. A call from the nursing home. You may have seen an ambulance outside my house just now. A young girl. Heart problems. I've placed her in my nursing home."

"You mean Mary Latimer?" asked Houston quickly.

Dr. Spedro looked at him in surprise. "You know her?"

"I don't, but my daughter who drove me here does. As it happens, we arrived just as the girl was being carried out into the ambulance. She doesn't seem to be doing very well."

"You're right about that, Inspector. A matter of the heart, as I said. Mary Latimer suffered a severe collapse here in my consulting room earlier. I always expected something like this would happen to her one day. But unfortunately she didn't listen to my advice. If I could have treated her thoroughly in time..." He raised his hands, as if at a loss. "But she didn't want to admit that she was suffering badly. Now it may be too late."

"I'm sorry to hear that," Houston said. He hesitated for a moment. "It could be that my daughter would like to visit the patient."

"I don't think that's possible," Dr Spedro replied. "But if you call me sometime tomorrow – maybe – maybe I can tell you more then."

Houston nodded. "And as for your car, doctor – I'll have it brought back here tomorrow."

He took his leave. Dr Spedro watched him go until the door closed behind him.

On his way to the exit, Houston passed the waiting room. The door was open. In passing, Houston glanced inside. He saw a waiting man off to the side and recognised him. Quickly, so that the man in the waiting room wouldn't notice him, Houston carried on. It surprised him to find this man here. But there was no mistake about who it was.

The next person Dr Spedro would receive that evening, the man in the waiting room, was Sir Cedric Kelford. The father of little Susan, who had been lured and abducted by a criminal with a yellow windmill. Spedro also owned a yellow windmill. And now Sir Cedric Kelford was here... But as a patient?

***

"There you are at last!" Rona welcomed her father.

"I'm afraid it took a little longer than I expected," Houston said, pulling the car door shut and remaining silent until Rona started up the engine.

"By the way, Rona! I'd like to make a few more enquiries here in the neighbourhood about this Spedro and his nursing home. I'd prefer it if we had a quick meal around here."

"I know a little restaurant on Devonshire Street," Rona said. "It's not far from here at all. I went there once with Carl."

As they ate, she quietly told her father what had happened that afternoon. She concealed the fact that a truck had tried to hit her car on the Albert Bridge. She didn't want to worry him. And the more she thought about the incident, doubts came back to her as to whether it had actually been intentional.

"Strange that Mary Latimer should know Carl Knight," Houston mused. "I wonder if Carl didn't also know Dennis better than we've assumed so far."

"But they hardly ever exchanged more than a dozen words," Rona objected.

"As far as we know," Houston said.

"And what's that supposed to mean?"

He paid the bill and looked at his watch. "It's pretty late already. I don't know how much longer I'm going to need. I think, Rona, it's better if you go home now, after all. Go home and get yourself to bed. Think of all those exhausting rehearsals you still have to do!"

***

Shortly after ten o'clock, Rona was home. She was about to undress when she heard a car pull up in front of the house.

A few seconds later, someone knocked on the front door. She zipped up her dress and went to the door. The experiences of that day had made her cautious. She put the security chain on first before opening the door a little. "Who is it?" she asked.

"It's me, Carl."

She unfastened the chain and let him in.

"I'm sorry, Rona, for being such a pig to you this afternoon. But I have so much on my mind at the moment."

He dropped into an armchair and buried his chin in his hands. He looked pale and strained. I actually feel sorry for him, Rona thought.

"By the way – was I mistaken, or...?" She told him that she thought she recognised him with Mary Latimer in the entrance to a shopping arcade. Knight's cheek muscles tightened.

"You're wrong, Rona," he said quietly. "I haven't seen that girl since you introduced me to her in the cafeteria. I went straight to my flat after I left you."

Rona dropped the subject. She'd driven over in the car. The man's back had been half turned to her. There were hundreds, probably thousands of men of Carl Knight's stature. She could have been mistaken.

Carl Knight continued to speak, but Rona, absorbed in her reflections, barely listened to him. Only when he mentioned her brother's name did she look at him intently.

"You must get your father to give up this Kelford case," Carl said. "He could be in terrible danger if he continues. My

God, you don't want to lose him too, Rona! Think of what happened to Dennis!"

"He's already been given the opportunity to withdraw from the case. But he wants to solve it himself, even if it costs him the rest of his life."

Carl Knight stood up and reached for his hat. "If that's the case, I don't know what else can be done to stop him. If you can't manage it..."

His imploring tone fell on Rona's nerves. "But why should I do that, Carl? I would do the same in his place. I'll even help him as much as I can," she said irritably.

To ease the tension between them a little, she offered him a drink. Carl declined.

"I wish you'd tell me the real reason you're dramatising all this," she said, "Maybe I could help."

"I just came to warn you, Rona. Surely there's no question of dramatising. This isn't a play. It's reality. And I mean, all these things are serious and dangerous enough."

Rona shook her head. "Carl," she said forcefully. "You don't have anything to do with this case at all. So why are you trying to convince me that I have to get my father to give it up? I just don't understand."

"I can't tell you exactly why." Knight shrugged. "Call it a feeling, call it an intuition, call it a premonition – whatever you want! I just mean..."

"I'm sorry you made the trip here in vain," Rona interrupted him.

Carl Knight turned away and headed for the door. "Let's forget it! Maybe I overdid it too – will I see you at the studio tomorrow?"

She nodded and wished him goodnight.

"Good night, Rona."

She watched him go down the stairs, then slowly closed the door.

42

The clock in the hallway struck eleven. High time I went to bed, Rona thought, I have a busy day tomorrow.

On the way to her room, she had to pass her brother Dennis's room. The door was closed. Rona hadn't entered the room since the evening Dennis was murdered. But she knew exactly what was in it.

The oak bed with the reading lamp, the desk on which lay the textbooks Dennis had used for his advanced course, the school photographs on the walls. It was all so normal and everyday. Who could have gained anything by killing Dennis, a harmless young man? And yet: he'd been murdered!

Rona was tired, but she couldn't sleep. Suddenly she sat up in bed. There'd been a noise. Like a door being closed. She switched on the bedside lamp and looked at the clock. It was a quarter to two.

Her father had come back at last, Rona thought. She threw on a dressing gown and left her room. There was another noise. It came from her brother's room! As if something had fallen to the floor. Rona hesitated for a moment, then pushed open the door and felt for the light switch. Before she reached it, two hands closed around her throat. Rona gasped. She squirmed and pushed with her elbows behind her. She heard the other breathing heavily. Desperately she tried to pull the hands from her neck. She screamed. But her scream was stifled. The stranglehold around her neck tightened, and tightened more. Blood roared in her ears as she tried with her last strength to free herself. From below, she heard the sound of the front door. Then quick steps on the stairs. The burglar flung Rona to the floor, rushed to the window and yanked it open.

"Rona – where are you?" she heard her father call out, as if from far away. A cold breeze from the window brought her back to her senses. Trembling, she straightened up. "Here," she called, "here in Dennis's room!"

43

Houston switched on the light.

"My God, Rona! What's happened?"

She pointed to the open window. Houston quickly glanced there and bent down to help her up.

"I'm all right, Dad," she brought out, still struggling. Houston ran to the window and looked out. He closed it and ran out of the flat down the stairs. He searched the garden. He couldn't find a trace of anyone.

When he returned, Rona was sitting in the living room. She was sipping a glass of brandy. Houston put an arm around her and stroked her back. "Now, calm down first, love. And then tell me..."

"I feel better already," Rona said. "There's not much to tell."

"So you didn't see him at all?" asked Houston, when she had finished her brief explanation.

"The room was dark. And I never got around to turning on the light."

Houston walked over to his son's room. It had been ransacked. Items were not in their usual places. But as far as Houston could tell, nothing was missing. He turned and saw Rona standing in the doorway.

"Who on earth could it have been?" asked Houston.

"All I know is that it was a man," said Rona. "I realised it when I struggled."

"Maybe a petty opportunist," said Houston. "Don't get too upset about it anymore, Rona. Try to get some sleep now. You have to be back at the studio by eight o'clock..."

He walked her up to her room.

"What did you find out about Dr Spedro, Dad?"

"Not much. He seems to be a heart specialist, with a very prosperous practice. This nursing home, I'm told, he's only recently taken it over."

"And you didn't find out anything about Mary Latimer?"

Mike Houston patted his daughter on the shoulder. "All in good time. Come – take a pill and try to sleep."

Maybe a petty opportunist burglar, he had said to Rona. But he didn't believe it.

***

Mike Houston had already eaten breakfast when Rona appeared. He asked her if he could have her car. "Then tonight I'll come to the studio to see the rerun of your play."

Just as he was about to leave the house, the postman arrived and Houston returned once more to his flat to hand Rona a large envelope.

She tore open the envelope. "Why, it's my play manuscript!" she exclaimed. "I must have left it in the cafeteria yesterday."

"Good thing someone sent it to you. I'm just wondering how the person in question got your address?" asked Houston,

"Maybe from the phone book," guessed Rona.

"Could be," Houston muttered and left.

Rona ate breakfast, then reached for the script to review some scenes. She turned the first page. Her breath caught in her throat. Scrawled on the blank space above the first line were a few words: "There will be a third fatality if your father doesn't give up the Kelford case." Below that, a crude sketch. A sketch of a windmill.

***

Rona had phoned for a taxi. As she entered the small cafeteria, she looked around searchingly. The room was almost empty.

"Can I speak to the owner, please?"

The girl behind the counter called out to him. Rona asked him her questions.

"I don't know anything about a play manuscript," he assured her. "Probably someone found it and took it."

Twenty minutes later, in the studio, she asked the director, Terry Smith. He didn't know anything about the manuscript either, and when he looked at the envelope, he explained that there was no way it could have been returned by the television company.

"But come on now, Rona," the director said. "We have to rehearse thoroughly again so that everything goes without a hitch tonight."

***

After the show, Rona quickly removed her make-up. She found her father in the large room from which visitors to the studio can watch the broadcasts.

"I'm so proud of you," Houston said with a smile.

"Did you see it all?"

"All except for the first few minutes. I've had a lot to do today."

"Let's go home, Dad," Rona urged. "I have something important to tell you."

"Me too," Houston said.

After the heat in the television studio, the evening air seemed cold. Rona shivered as she walked beside her father down the street to the small cul-de-sac where Houston had parked the car.

In the glow of the streetlights, Houston looked tired and haggard, Rona thought. He had visibly aged in the last few weeks.

The cul-de-sac was only sparsely lit. The low-rise houses on either side of the short road lay in darkness. Mike Houston put the key in the door lock of the car and pulled the handle. At that moment, he felt a weight pressing against the door from inside. Houston quickly looked in both directions of the deserted street.

"Get on the pavement, Rona! I think there's someone in the car."

46

As he spoke, he opened the door, reaching out to catch the human body that fell towards him. It was a woman. He braced himself against her and reached across her for the overhead light switch. He recognised her immediately.

"Who is it, Dad?" asked Rona behind him.

"Mary Latimer!" groaned Houston. "Come and help me!"

"There's blood on her face!" exclaimed Rona. But Mike Houston was staring at Mary Latimer's left hand. Her fingers were tangled around something he had seen before. It was a yellow windmill. The yellow windmill from Dr Spedro's consulting room.

Chapter Four

The blood on Mary Latimer's face glistened. Wet and dark. Rona Houston shuddered. She turned away from the slender figure slumped in the front seat of the car.

It hasn't been twenty-four hours, Rona thought, since she called me and wanted to talk to me privately. That never happened – and now....

Whatever Mary Latimer had wanted to tell her – she wouldn't have another chance to reveal it now.

Mary Latimer was dead. Inspector Mike Houston hadn't said a word as his daughter looked at the motionless figure in her car. He heard Rona breathing rapidly. He looked up and down the dark side alley – no one was to be seen.

Houston asked his daughter to call the nearest police station from a phonebox. "Tell them to make sure an ambulance is sent here, too!"

When Rona had moved away, he carefully pulled something out of Mary Latimer's left hand. It was the little yellow windmill. Houston took it and walked with it into the circle of light coming from a streetlamp. He was still examining the model when Rona returned.

"Where did you get that?" she asked in surprise.

"Mary Latimer was holding it," Houston replied.

"What are you saying?" Rona too began to look closely at the windmill. "I didn't notice it earlier."

"You must have been too confused," Houston said. "You kept staring at her face."

Houston lifted the windmill a little closer to his face and looked over it into his daughter's eyes. "I've seen one just like this before," he said quietly.

"Where?" Rona's eyes widened.

"On a shelf in Dr Spedro's consulting room. I..."

48

Mike Houston wanted to give Rona more explanation, but he didn't get to it. A police patrol car, followed by an ambulance, arrived.

Houston acquainted himself with the policemen and briefed them on the details of what had happened.

The men from the ambulance put the dead girl on a stretcher and transported her away. Ten minutes later, Houston and Rona drove home.

"I just want to know what she was doing in my car?" asked Rona after a long silence while her father drove the car through the heavy evening traffic.

Houston shrugged. "She'll have been waiting for one of us, I suppose."

"But I can't imagine how she managed to leave the nursing home. I thought they said she was seriously ill!"

"We only have Dr Spedro's word for that," Houston objected. "I'm interested in what the autopsy says. Whether she really had a heart condition or not..."

Rona cast a quick sideways glance at him. He didn't seem to trust Dr Spedro too much.

"How could someone manage to murder her there, in the open street?" asked Rona.

"It wouldn't be that difficult," Houston interrupted her. "Someone was following her, someone with some kind of stiletto knife. And that someone waited for the right moment. When there was no one on the street but him and his victim. The cul-de-sac was dark. And all the rest – for a certain kind of person would be quite easy..."

After they had crossed Hammersmith Bridge, Rona asked, "When you picked me up at the studio earlier, Dad, you said that you had something else to tell me. What was it?"

"Just that I visited Dr Spedro's nursing home again this afternoon. I found that Mary Latimer had left the home. The sister told me that Mary Latimer had recovered remarkably quickly."

"At least that explains why she was already able to walk around and wait for us."

He nodded, then looked at the dashboard clock. "I've got to get a move on. I asked Bob Harridge to be with us at ten. And it's getting on for twenty to already."

"Bob Harridge?" asked Rona in amazement. "What do you want with him?"

"My colleague Inspector Loman – you know him – caught up with some research. And he found out that our Dennis met Mary Latimer quite often. It was Bob Harridge who introduced them to each other. I think Bob can explain a few things to us. He may shed a little more light on this whole affair!"

As they approached Roehampton Road, Rona decided to tell her father about the mysterious note she'd found in the returned play manuscript.

"This is the third time we've been threatened in case you don't give up the investigation," she reminded him.

He turned to her and smiled briefly.

"I've had a lot of warnings like that in my life," he said, his eyes on the road. "It's just part of the job. I've never taken threats like that very seriously."

He hesitated for a moment before continuing: "By the way, about your friend Carl Knight, I don't know... I'd rather you didn't see him for a while. In fact, I think it would be a good idea for you to visit Aunt Kitty for a few days. You could do with a bit of a rest, Rona, and I'm sure the air there in Dorset will do you good."

Rona shook her head decisively. "Now that you're in the middle of this difficult case, you want me to leave you alone? Out of the question, Dad! After all, Dennis was my brother.

And if I can be of the slightest use in this matter, I can't just run away. That's what I said to Carl, too."

"And what did Carl say about that?" asked Houston.

"He was quite beside himself. He tried to make me understand that the fact that you were involved in the Kelford case had already cost the life of one of our family. And he said there may be others..."

"Did you ask him what made him think like that?"

"He wouldn't tell me..."

Mike Houston took her hand. "You're a good kid," he said softly. "Your mother would have been as proud of you as I am today. Don't you worry, Rona! We'll get this case sorted out. And maybe it won't even take that long..."

When they arrived home, Bob Harridge's car was in their drive. Bob was pacing up and down in front of the house.

Mike Houston quickly got out and apologised. "Sorry to keep you waiting so long."

"That's all right, sir," Bob assured Harridge. "I've been taking in the night air. It's good for me, too!"

He followed Houston and Rona into the house.

Houston invited him into the living room. "Have a seat please!" He drew the curtains and turned back to Bob. "Pretty chilly in here, don't you think?" He switched on an electric heater. Rona meanwhile took off her hat and coat in the hallway and combed her hair. When she stepped into the room, her father had just told the young bank clerk about Mary Latimer's death.

"But what does it all mean, Mr Houston?" asked Bob Harridge excitedly. "And what's behind it all?"

"That's what I want to know," Houston replied calmly. "And that's also the reason I asked you here tonight, Bob. I thought you might be able to help me shed a little light on a dark spot or two."

51

Bob Harridge shook his head. "I wish I could," he said and heaved a sigh. "But I'm in the dark too. The people at the bank have asked me all sorts of questions. But I haven't been able to tell them much. Mary Latimer met Dennis and I on the same occasion – at a dance. I think he met her a couple of times later, but I didn't bother about it any further. The girl didn't interest me. Not my type at all."

"Did you see Mary again?" asked Houston.

Harridge nodded. "Four of us went to the theatre once or twice – Dennis, Mary, me and Cynthia Harper from our West End branch. But if I remember rightly, I hardly spoke to Mary Latimer for more than a few minutes. I don't even remember what it was about."

"Then why did you meet her in that cafeteria?" interjected Rona.

Bob Harridge frowned. "Yes, that's such a strange thing too. Mary Latimer called me at the office and asked me to meet her. She had something important to tell me about Dennis. As you know, Rona, we met in that cafeteria. But until you came she didn't say a word about Dennis, and neither did she while you were there. Later, when I went to ask her about it, she suddenly acted as if she were in a hurry, saying she had something very urgent to do, and she rushed off. Just left me there and disappeared!"

Houston and Rona had listened attentively to Bob's story. "Strange," muttered Mike Houston. "Very strange..."

"Were you the one who sent my manuscript back to me?" asked Rona, looking at Bob Harridge.

He raised his eyebrows in wonder. "What manuscript, Rona? I haven't seen one. Do you mean in the café?"

"I'm not sure where I left it," Rona said, perplexed. "I suppose it's also possible I lost it in the street somewhere."

Mike Houston drummed the fingers of his right hand on the arm of the chair. "So you don't know anything else about this Mary Latimer either, Bob?" he asked. "Nor what she did for a living? Was she employed somewhere, do you know?"

"She never said a word about that to me," Bob Harridge hastily assured him. "Somehow she always gave me the impression that she was a bit of an erratic type, if you know what I mean. She seemed so restless and thoroughly unconventional. She wasn't bad, that's not it. But I always wondered why a man like Dennis, of all people, was so interested in her – at least it seemed that way to me," he added.

Rona gave her father a quick glance. "It's possible that's why he never brought her home here," she said quietly.

Bob Harridge looked from one to the other and lowered his head before continuing. "As far as Dennis and Mary Latimer were concerned, I never quite got rid of a certain feeling."

He faltered and seemed to be searching for words. "You know, the other young people in the bank, they like to talk about their girlfriends and brag a bit too, you know.... Dennis though – he never said a word about Mary Latimer. He never mentioned her, I know that for a fact. It was as if she didn't exist. So he kept quiet about her, if I may call it that. And that gave me the idea..."

"Yes?" interjected Houston.

Bob Harridge squirmed. Apparently he was rather uncomfortable with the point the conversation had reached.

"Well," he said at last, "I was wondering whether she might be – how shall I put it? – whether Mary Latimer might have had some sort of hold over him, as it were. It needn't have been anything serious, but I wondered sometimes..."

He turned to Houston. "Dennis could be quite secretive, sir, as you will know. Even more so now that it's apparently established that he never mentioned the girl to you in a single word either."

"Yes, he was a little shy," Rona said, nodding. "He never spoke to us about his most private matters. Not even in a hint about what was going on."

"As I said – he was cagey," Bob Harridge continued. "And so, apart from a few impressions, which I'm sure are not very revealing, I can't tell you anything about this matter. I've told you all I know, sir, and I'm sorry I can't help you a little more. After all, the whole affair seems to be getting more and more mysterious."

Houston nodded. "Anyway, I'd be very grateful to you, Bob, if you'd keep your eyes and ears open in the future. Let me know anything that might be the least bit important!"

"Of course, sir," Bob stood up.

"I'll take you down," Houston said.

"And I'll come with you," Rona explained. "I forgot something in the car."

Mike Houston opened the front door. He squinted his eyes. After the bright lighting in the hallway, the night outside seemed pitch black.

Bob Harridge stood beside him. "So goodbye then," he turned to Rona, who was waiting behind him for him and her father to step out into the night.

At that moment it happened. A car engine howled. There were three crashes. Mike Houston heard a bullet whistle, close above his head. It smacked into somewhere....

Houston yanked Harridge back in a flash. Rona screamed. Then it was over. The car disappeared into the darkness of the night. Bob Harridge clutched the post at the foot of the stairs. He looked pale.

"Are you all right, Bob?" asked Houston quickly.

Harridge muttered something.

"Come on, we'd best get back to the flat," Houston said.

***

54

"Was that one shot, or was it several?" asked Rona, who had already calmed down. The experiences of the last few days had accustomed her to surprises, even dangerous ones.

"I couldn't tell," said Houston. "My eyes hadn't adjusted enough to the darkness. I saw a hand, the hand with the gun. That was all, and even that only for seconds or fractions of a second. The car was speeding along like crazy!"

They were back in the living room. Houston reached for the whisky bottle. "Bring us some glasses, Rona. I think we could all do with a sip after that scare. Like targets, we stood in the brightly lit doorway. It's a wonder no one got hit!"

Slowly the colour returned to Bob Harridge's face.

"Don't worry," Houston reassured him. "We're at peace for tonight. It never actually happens that twice in one evening an attempt is made..." He interrupted himself. "But I'll order a police car here to escort you home!"

He left the room to make a phone call.

When the patrol car stopped in front of the house, Houston went out to make sure the coast was clear. Then Bob Harridge left the house and drove off, followed by the police car.

"Poor Bob," Rona said as Houston thoughtfully returned to the living room. "He's taken a lot out of all this, don't you think? I don't think he'll be back here with us any time soon. One other thing I wanted to ask you – did you recognise the car earlier?"

"It was a big dark sedan," Houston explained calmly.

"One thing I don't understand," Rona said. "If someone was following you, why, in order for him to fire his shots, would he have waited until you opened the front door? How would he even know if you were going to leave the house again tonight?"

Houston looked at his daughter. "I don't think I was shot at either."

Incredulous, Rona opened her mouth, "You mean the shots were aimed..."

"I think there is a strong case to be made that Bob Harridge was the target," her father affirmed.

***

The Detective Superintendent pushed aside the stack of reports on his desk.

"I have studied these reports very thoroughly, my dear Houston, and I cannot but conclude..." He hesitated.

"You mean to say that it appears that my son Dennis was in some way involved with the organisation you suspect of kidnapping Susan Kelford?" Mike Houston's voice sounded firm and matter-of-fact.

The Superintendent nodded. "Certain facts seem to point in that direction. Are you sure, Houston, that you want to pursue this case further? I mean..."

"Quite sure," Houston interrupted him. "If it is to be confirmed that Dennis was connected with this case, I am the most suitable man to lead this investigation."

"You're right," the Superintendent admitted. "I know we can rely on you, Mike," he continued quietly in a confidential tone. "I just wanted to spare your personal feelings in case there was anything that..."

"That's very kind of you, sir. But if I had been taken off this case – I would have taken my leave and investigated further on my own."

"All right, Houston. No need to get dramatic. You're staying with us. That's all we need, you of all people..." The Superintendent rose and squeezed Mike Houston's hand firmly.

***

Ten minutes later, Houston was on his way to see Dr Spedro, with whom he had made an appointment as a precaution. He was shown into the waiting room. To his disappointment, the doctor received him there and didn't call him into the consulting room.

Houston immediately got to the point and asked how it was possible that Mary Latimer was already fit enough to leave the hospital when she had had to be taken there on a stretcher less than twenty-four hours previously.

Spedro shrugged. "You can never tell with heart attacks, Inspector."

"Was she then under the influence of drugs when she was taken to the home?"

"Certainly not. I told you she collapsed here in the consulting room."

"If she felt so bad, why did they let her go?"

"I think she was able to leave without anyone noticing. You know, Inspector, that we can't force a patient to stay. If someone decides to leave, they leave."

Houston had to admit that the doctor's answers sounded plausible. Still, Spedro's way of dodging answers made him a little suspicious.

"Would you tell me how it came about that she consulted you?" he asked.

"Gladly. Another patient of mine, Sir Cedric Kelford, recommended me."

Something clicked inside Houston.

"Was she a friend of Sir Cedric's then?" he enquired.

"I have no idea. But no doubt he can tell you."

"How long has he been consulting you?"

"For about three months. Lately he has been visiting me often. I suppose you know that his little daughter has been kidnapped. Worries about her have made his heart condition much worse."

In the consulting room, the phone rang and Spedro went to answer it. Houston followed him into the hallway.

Suddenly the consulting room door opened and Spedro said, "Scotland Yard would like to speak to you."

As he went to the telephone, which was by the window, Houston tried to hide the fact that he was glancing at the mantelpiece. He heard Spedro close the door and instinctively turned. The yellow windmill was still there. So it obviously couldn't be the same one that Mary Latimer was clutching when she was murdered.

Inspector Loman was on the other end of the line and told Houston that Sir Cedric Kelford wanted to see him urgently. Then Houston heard Loman hang up. He himself waited a moment before taking the receiver from his ear to put it on the hook.

And what he had expected happened: There was a crackling sound on the line! Houston knew the sound. Someone had overheard the conversation between him and Loman from an extension.

As Houston stepped out into the hall, Dr Spedro was coming down the stairs.

"I have to go now," Houston said. "Just one more thing, doctor. You will have to be a witness at the coroner's inquest. Mary Latimer was your patient, after all." He told him the time and place.

They said goodbye to each other. Dr Spedro looked Houston straight in the eye. Mike Houston decided to go straight to Sir Cedric Kelford's house.

The bank president lived in an elegant house in Eaton Square. On the way there, Houston thought about his visit to Dr Spedro. What was he to make of the doctor?

Certainly Spedro wasn't the conventional type of the well-behaved family doctor. He seemed to be more of a "fashionable doctor", and certainly there were patients in certain circles who found it "chic" to be treated by Dr Spedro. In addition, the doctor's appearance was rather exotic.

He seems somewhat inscrutable, Houston thought. But he had to admit to himself that Spedro's statements about Mary Latimer's illness were true. The post-mortem report stated that Mary Latimer had indeed suffered from heart disease.

***

Houston was immediately taken to Sir Cedric Kelford's study. Even before the banker greeted him, Houston realised that Kelford was very agitated.

Kelford pointed to a sheet of paper lying on his desk. "Here, Inspector! Read this!"

Houston stepped up beside him and bent over the sheet to read. He didn't touch it.

"Your daughter is alive and well," the note read. It was typewritten. "If you wish to see her again, deposit £7000 in the telephone box at the end of Oasthouse Lane in Haydock Green on Saturday evening, ten o'clock. Wait near the phone box. Do not contact the police. Otherwise you will never see your child again."

The long-awaited ransom letter! Finally, Houston thought. Maybe it will give us a new lead. Kelford looked at him eagerly.

"Can I see the envelope too, sir?" asked Houston.

He scrutinised the envelope, caught the letter with a pair of tweezers lying on the desk and slid it into the envelope.

"Give me the letter, sir," Houston said. "Maybe we can do something with it. I'll call you about it again today. You haven't spoken to anyone about this, have you?"

Kelford shook his head. "Of course I haven't. But I'm relying entirely on you, Houston. Nothing can go wrong as far as Susan is concerned. You know – I needn't have notified you about that letter. I could have simply paid, and..."

"But you are mistaken if you think you'll get Susan back as easily as the ransom letter promises," Houston explained.

***

After leaving Kelford, Houston drove back to Scotland Yard and handed the ransom note over to the fingerprint specialists. He was still briefing Inspector Loman on the latest developments when the phone rang again. Rona was on the line. "I'm going into town now, Dad. Carl just called me and told me that Ambrose Wyler is interested in the TV broadcast and he wants me to play my part for him too," she gushed.

"And who exactly is Ambrose Wyler?" asked Houston.

"Oh, come on, Dad! You know – the well-known theatre producer."

"Oh, yes," Houston said quickly. "I remember now. And he wants to put on the television play with you in it on the stage? I'm glad to hear it."

Suddenly a new thought occurred to him. She had been talking about Carl. Carl Knight.

"Just a minute, Rona," Houston said. "There's something else I wanted to ask – do you happen to have a letter from your friend Knight written on his typewriter?"

"Yes, I think I still have a movie synopsis he sent me once. He told me he typed it up himself."

"Can you drop it off here at the Yard when you come to town, Rona? Put it in an envelope and address it to me personally. I'll have the letter picked up from downstairs."

"I'll be there as soon as I can," Rona assured him and hung up.

***

The offices of theatre producer Ambrose Wyler were housed in a new building in St James Street. Rona arrived ten minutes early. Excited by the prospect of playing her part on stage, she paced restlessly in the elegantly furnished waiting room.

Suddenly the door opened and a man in a chauffeur's uniform entered.

"Miss Houston?"

"Yes," Rona said in amazement. "Can I help you?"

"I'm sorry, Miss Houston," the chauffeur said. "But your father..."

An icy horror ran through Rona. "What's wrong with him?" she groaned.

"It's nothing serious, miss," the man reassured her. "Really, not. Just a little incident. But he was asking for you. Could you perhaps..."

"Yes, but of course," Rona exclaimed.

"I have a car outside," said the man in the chauffeur's uniform. "It won't take more than ten minutes."

Rona's heart beat wildly as she followed him down the stairs.

She had arranged to meet her father at Danilo's restaurant at seven in the evening. But now...

"Are you sure it's nothing serious?" she asked the chauffeur.

"The doctor assured me there was no cause for concern, miss," he replied politely. "And I believe him."

He opened the door of a large black Cadillac and held it open for Rona.

It was only when the chauffeur had closed the door that Rona noticed someone sitting in the back.

The man was leaning in the corner. Now he leaned forward. Rona looked at him with wide eyes. The man smiled.

"I don't believe I've had the pleasure of being introduced to you, Miss Houston," he said.

At that moment, before he could even give his name, she recognised him.

It was Dr Spedro!

Chapter Five

She knew it was too late. She couldn't get out of the car. The driver had quickly slid behind the wheel of the huge Cadillac and accelerated.

She stared at the small, rather dark-skinned man in the back seat and tried to control herself despite the fear rising inside her. What was he going to do with her?

He looked at her calmly. "Your father may have mentioned my name to you perhaps, Miss Houston – I'm Dr Spedro."

Rona could only nod. She couldn't get a word out.

"I must apologise for that little deception, my dear," Dr Spedro continued. "Please, don't be upset! Nothing at all has happened to your father. As far as I know, he's fine."

Rona could barely keep herself together. She considered rolling down the window and screaming for help. But surely she wouldn't get away with it. There was Spedro, and there was the driver. All that was left for her to do for the moment was to resign herself to whatever happened in the following minutes.

"What do you want from me?" she asked angrily.

"Don't be angry, Miss Houston. I just want us to have a little conversation. I suggest we drive around St James's Park for ten minutes. Ten minutes... that will suffice."

Rona was silent, and apparently Spedro interpreted her silence as agreement. He gave the driver a wave and the man nodded and turned into the wide bend at the beginning of St James Street.

"Your father seems to be under the impression that I am in some way involved in the murder of a man named Nobbler Williams," Spedro continued.

"I'm sorry," Rona said coolly. "But my father isn't in the habit of discussing his professional affairs with me."

"Surely he made an exception in this case," Dr Spedro insisted. "Can I have misunderstood him – or did he say that Mary Latimer was a friend of yours?"

"A friend? Hardly. She knew my brother."

Her dismissive tone didn't escape him. "I'm just trying to help the police," he said. "I've told them everything I know about Mary Latimer. I'm afraid it wasn't much. But I can't help that. Has your father found any clue yet as to who the murderer might be?"

Rona gave him a sharp look in which she tried to put all her reluctance. "I've already explained to you, Doctor, that my father doesn't talk to me about such things. And if he did – I don't see why I should take you into my confidence. Why don't you ask him yourself if you want to know something!" Rona talked herself into a rage.

"But Miss Houston!"

"Oh, stop it, Doctor! Why are you so interested in this case anyway? Just because the girl was your patient? Or do you have some other reason?"

The driver pretended not to hear any of this. Silently, he concentrated on the traffic.

Dr Spedro didn't take his eyes off Rona as he pulled the lunch edition of a newspaper from his coat pocket. He unfolded it and held it so that Rona could see the first page. In the headline was the name Mary Latimer.

"Maybe you'll read what's in this article," Spedro said, thrusting the paper into Rona's hand.

Rona read. The writer of the report suggested that the yellow windmill Mary Latimer had been holding when she died might give the police an important lead. He had also found out that after the murder of Dennis Houston, a drawing of a yellow windmill had been found on the television set in the Houstons' living room. The journalist connected the two cases and made all sorts of connections and assumptions.

Rona Houston looked up and had the feeling that Dr Spedro had been watching her incessantly while she read. She handed the newspaper back to him. He threw the paper on the seat beside him without looking at it.

"Your father has discovered that there is a yellow windmill in my consulting room, Miss Houston," Dr Spedro said quietly and insistently. "He seemed to attach a lot of importance to that fact. He acted a little strangely, if I may say so. He didn't ask direct questions, but talked around it. I couldn't make sense of it. But now, of course, after reading this article, I realise why he was so interested in my little yellow windmill."

"All right," said Rona, still annoyed. "Then why don't you go and tell him all about it?"

Dr Spedro leaned forward. Rona backed away a little.

"My dear young lady, there is nothing to tell. My model of a yellow windmill is only a souvenir. I brought it back from a short visit to Amsterdam. That's all."

"Then I don't know what you're so worried about," Rona said dismissively.

"You will understand that at once, Miss Houston! I wish your father would finally realise that I am a respected doctor with a reputation to lose. I simply cannot afford to have the police coming in and out of my house. And I certainly don't want to be involved in or associated with any dubious affairs. You must understand that! What will my patients think when they find out that I have..."

Rona was suddenly at a loss. Much of what Dr Spedro had said made sense to her. The seriousness with which he spoke impressed her.

"My father's always very careful before he makes accusations," she said quietly. "But if you think it is right – very well, I will tell him what you've told me."

Dr Spedro bowed politely. "That's all I wanted, Miss Houston. Thank you." He glanced through the car window. "I see we are already back near the office we picked you up from. I hope you'll forgive me for the little ruse I used to lure you into this car. But I saw no other way. As you now know, it was all quite harmless."

He said goodbye with many apologies to Rona, who reacted a little more kindly but remained cool.

She got out in front of the large office building where the theatre director Ambrose Wyler presided. She stopped for a moment at the edge of the pavement to watch the big Cadillac slowly drive away. A strange man, this Dr Spedro, she thought as she walked towards the entrance of the office building.

She looked at her watch. Despite the unscheduled ride with Spedro, she was still on time for her appointment with Wyler.

She pressed the lift button and followed the signal lights on the indicator board when she heard quick footsteps behind her. A hand touched her elbow. She wheeled around. Behind her stood Carl Knight. He looked pale and tense.

"Whose car was that?" he asked quickly. His eyes flickered.

It took Rona a few seconds to recover from her surprise. She looked at Carl intently. "It belongs to a Dr Spedro," she said then. "Why do you want to know?"

Carl Knight didn't answer her question. "Who's he? What do you know about him?" he wanted to know.

Rona frowned. "Practically nothing. He was Mary Latimer's doctor. That's why he wanted to know from me if

65

my father had discovered any trace of her killer yet. But what's it to you, Carl?"

Carl Knight forced himself to smile. "I'm sorry, Rona. But I was worried about you. You really shouldn't be so careless as to let strangers take you off in their cars. You never know..."

"You're exaggerating, Carl."

He glanced at her wristwatch. "Come on!" The lift doors slid apart. "We mustn't keep the great theatre director waiting," Carl Knight said.

***

The report from Scotland Yard's experts turned out as Mike Houston had expected. The ransom letter to Sir Cedric Kelford and Carl Knight's film manuscript, which Rona had obtained for her father, were written on the same typewriter!
Throughout the afternoon, Houston tried to reach the playwright. He called Knight's flat several times, but no one answered.

Houston thought about it. He wanted to find Carl Knight as soon as possible to ask him some important questions. The most important one being: who besides Knight had access to that typewriter?

Mike Houston called the office of theatre director Ambrose Wyler. A secretary told him Knight had arrived around noon but soon left.

Finally, Wyler himself came on the line. "He was going to visit another movie studio, but please don't ask me which one. I can't remember. I think it was one of those that's pretty far out."

Inspector Mike Houston decided to make another attempt to find Knight later. He drove to Marylebone and made a few enquiries about Dr Spedro.

Ten minutes earlier than arranged with Rona, he arrived at Danilo's restaurant that evening. He went to the phone booth and called Sir Cedric Kelford.

"Have you heard anything new from Susan's kidnapper, Sir Cedric?"

"Not since the ransom letter arrived, Inspector."

"Very well, sir. We'll keep in touch. I've got some things to think about. May I call you again later?"

Sir Cedric Kelford agreed. "You can come here too, if you like."

Houston noted that his daughter looked very pleased as she entered the restaurant.

"Well, have you had any more attempts to persuade you to get me to give up the case?" he asked after they had ordered the food.

"Not that, Dad, but..."

She told him about her conversation with Dr Spedro and the way the doctor had lured her into his car. She could see that her father was very uncomfortable during her story.

"Actually, it's a pretty strong ploy about what Spedro got himself into," Mike Houston muttered.

"Did you find out anything new about him?" asked Rona.

Houston made a gruff motion with his hand. "As far as he's concerned, that's one of the most exhausting chapters of the whole thing! I frankly don't like this fellow at all. I don't like the look in his eye. Or the way he talks. He's always evasive, never catching on. I spent almost the whole afternoon making enquiries about him. But I couldn't find anything really suspicious. One or two big wigs in the clinics spoke very highly of him. Well, let's leave that for the moment. Right now, I'm more interested in your friend Carl Knight."

"Carl?" she repeated, slightly surprised. "I saw him at lunchtime in Ambrose Wyler's office. He was terribly nice and insisted that I should play the lead part if the play went ahead on stage."

"That's wonderful," Houston nodded. "I'll keep my fingers crossed for you."

"And afterwards," she continued, "Carl took me to lunch and we had a nice chat."

"Did he tell you where he was going after that?"

"He had an appointment at the film studios in Shepperton. Why?"

"Because I've been trying to get hold of him all afternoon."

"Is something wrong?"

"We thought he might be able to give us some clarity on one or two points, that's all. Loman's going to see him at his house tomorrow morning."

Rona looked worried. "That sounds like one of those phrases the police say when they think a statement from a certain person will lead to the arrest of a murderer. And actually, you know that person is actually the one they're looking for for the crime."

Houston laughed. "It's not that bad."

When they'd finished their meal, Houston was waiting for Rona in the somewhat cramped foyer of the restaurant when he happened to bump into Bob Harridge.

"Nice to meet you, Inspector," Harridge said. "I've something to tell you that might interest you. It's about Mary Latimer." They moved to a corner of the foyer where they couldn't so easily be heard. "I was having lunch in a pub called 'The Rising Sun', just beyond Cheapside, when I overheard the waiter talking to some regulars. They had read about Mary Latimer in the lunchtime edition. The waiter told me that she often stopped by there, although he didn't know her name. One or two regulars could remember her too. I don't know if this information's of any use to you, sir. But I thought you might be able to use it. It's possible, after all, that she went there to meet someone."

"I'm very grateful to you, Bob," Houston said.

"Ah, over there I see the man coming with whom I have an appointment here, sir. Well, goodbye," Harridge said quickly. "If I hear anything new, I'll call you." He disappeared into the pub with the other man.

When Rona returned, Houston asked her to drive him to Sir Cedric Kelford's flat. Rona dropped him off in front of the house and drove on.

Almost to his surprise, Houston was led by the butler not into Kelford's study but into the sitting room.

Sir Cedric Kelford was talking to a striking red-haired woman. She wore a light coat that obviously was expensive. Houston estimated her to be in her mid-forties. There were two empty wine glasses on a small table.

"Come in, Houston," Sir Cedric called, "Come in!"

He turned to the redhead. "May I introduce you to Inspector Houston, Mrs Spedro?"

If Houston was surprised at the mention of the name, he betrayed it with no emotion. He bowed, they chatted about the weather for a few minutes and then Mrs Spedro declared she had to go. She said goodbye and Sir Cedric Kelford walked her to the door.

"You know Dr Spedro by now, too," he said as he returned.

Houston nodded.

"He's a bit of an odd bird," Kelford said. "But a very impressive man in his own way. By the way, Mrs Spedro was a good friend of my wife's."

"Oh, that's why you're consulting him," Houston said, stretching.

Sir Cedric Kelford raised his head with a jerk. "How do you know that I..."

"He happened to mention it," Houston said in an indifferent tone. "He also told me that you had recommended him to Mary Latimer."

Kelford considered. "I'm familiar with the name, only..."

"It's in all the evening papers," Houston reminded him.

"That's right," Kelford exclaimed. "Of course. That girl who was murdered."

Houston looked at him sharply. "Excuse me, Sir Cedric, but it sounds as if you didn't know Mary Latimer at all."

Kelford shook his head. "But I didn't know her, Inspector."

"And you didn't recommend her to Dr Spedro either?"

Kelford became annoyed. "How could I when, as I've just told you, I didn't know the girl at all. I assure you, Inspector, I first heard her name when I read the evening papers today. Spedro must be mistaken."

Houston was silent. Dr Spedro had asserted that Mary Latimer had become his patient on Sir Cedric Kelford's recommendation with such certainty that it seemed inconceivable that he could have been mistaken. Or had he for some reason tried to divert Houston's thoughts to a possible connection between Mary Latimer and Sir Cedric Kelford? Or was Kelford lying when he denied having known Mary Latimer?

"Let's talk about something else," Houston heard Kelford say. "How do you envisage things going tomorrow, Inspector? Do you want me to pay the ransom? Or should I not?" His voice sounded impatient.

"We think it right that you should follow the kidnapper's instructions to the letter, sir," Houston said calmly. "Get the money from the bank and deposit it in the telephone box he indicated in Haydock Green. You are prepared to do that, aren't you?"

Kelford nodded vigorously. His cheek muscles tensed. "When I think of my little Susan, poor child, I'm ready to do anything, Inspector," he said grimly. "I just hope you'll make sure nothing goes wrong."

"We will take all possible precautions," Houston assured him. "Of course, the most important thing is that you don't tell anyone about the ransom letter."

Kelford raised his hands impatiently. "You can count on me, Inspector, not to tell a soul a single word about it. I want my child back, and soon. Who knows what else will happen if we don't act quickly now?"

As Houston left Kelford's house and walked along Eaton Square, he saw a figure approaching that looked familiar. She stepped into the glow of a streetlight, and he recognised her. It was Mrs Spedro.

"Good evening, Inspector," she opened the conversation with. "It's such a mild evening, mild for this time of year, I mean, and I thought it would do me good to get some more air."

As she walked beside him, Houston wondered if she had been waiting for him. But nothing in her chatter betrayed that she wanted anything from him. "Will you walk with me to the end of the street, Inspector? I can easily pick up a taxi there."

Houston agreed. They walked slowly. A very attractive woman, Houston thought, eyeing her surreptitiously from the side. At least in this respect, Dr Spedro seemed to have excellent taste.

Houston couldn't shake the feeling that Mrs Spedro wanted to tell him something but didn't dare to do it. He decided to ask her directly. "Was there something you wanted to say to me, Mrs Spedro?" he asked openly.

She hesitated for a moment but didn't try to be evasive.

"I know your family better than you think, Inspector," she said in a firm voice.

Houston was surprised but didn't betray it with a word.

"Dennis told me a lot about you," it came softly from her lips.

Houston stopped. "You knew Dennis?"

She looked at him searchingly. The wind played with her red hair. "Very well indeed, Inspector. You don't mind, do you?"

"No, no..."

Houston's mind fell into confusion for a moment.

"Just – you know, hardly a day goes by since Dennis died that I don't meet someone he was friends with. People he never mentioned to me. I ask myself what I actually knew about my own son. Quite frankly, it's a bit of an embarrassing question for a father, don't you think?"

"I don't know," she replied. "I don't have children so I can't judge. But..."

"Do you know anything that might shed some light on the dark connections surrounding my son's death?" he interrupted her.

Mrs Spedro shook her head. She turned up her collar. "Since the wind started, it's getting cooler than I expected, isn't it? ... No, Inspector, I don't think I can help you there. I'm more concerned about your daughter."

"About Rona? Why?"

Mrs Spedro looked up at him obliquely. "I believe she's in great danger. Can't you persuade her to go away for a few weeks?"

"I've already tried that – in vain, I'm sorry to say."

Mrs Spedro heaved a sigh when she heard his reply.

"And what makes you think my daughter is in danger?" asked Houston.

"Well, it stands to reason after Dennis was killed."

He let a pause occur and then continued, "There are a lot of people who want me to give up on this case, Mrs Spedro. I don't know if these people are thinking about my safety or more about their own. And your husband, Mrs Spedro, let me know today through my daughter that he doesn't wish to be harassed. It's all very confusing, and very puzzling..."

Mike Houston didn't know what drove him to pour out his heart to this woman who walked beside him through the night, to reveal his feelings to her, his worries, his discomfort, his difficulties and his perplexity. He felt a strange trust in her. He wouldn't have been able to justify it if he'd been asked.

Before they reached the street corner, he asked, "How did you meet Dennis?"

"That question is quickly answered." Her dark voice sounded warm and full. "I was his teacher at the business school he attended at night. And he, he was my favourite student..."

"Really? You were his..." Houston broke off.

"Don't I look it, or what did you think?" chuckled Mrs Spedro. "I may not be the type of what you think of as a teacher. But I am one. If you're still interested – Dennis was a very promising student. I think he would have had quite a career ahead of him. At the end of the previous semester, I gave him a book of mine that had just been published: 'Economics Today' it's called."

Houston remained silent. He saw a taxi coming around the corner and waved. The car stopped. Houston helped Mrs Spedro into it.

"What I wanted to say – if your husband ever wants to talk to Rona again, he needn't plan it so dramatically again," he explained.

"I'll see to that," she said firmly. "But you'll have to forgive him, Inspector. He's quite excitable and prone to exaggeration. That's just his nature."

73

He watched the taxi until the tail lights disappeared and made his way to the next bus stop. He couldn't get the encounter with Mrs Spedro out of his mind.

She seemed to be a smart, warm-hearted woman. And obviously she had considerable knowledge of human nature. He admitted to himself that he liked her, unlike her husband.

**

Houston sucked on his pipe and thought again about the day's events. Dr Spedro's behaviour seemed mysterious, but offered no clues. The ransom letter to Sir Cedric Kelford had been written on Carl Knight's typewriter. But that was no evidence against Knight. It's a pity I never got hold of him, Houston thought. He regretted that this line of inquiry was still unfinished.

When Houston got home, Rona was standing in the kitchen. A stimulating aroma of coffee greeted him. "I'll be right there, Dad." He went ahead into the living room, she following him with the coffee tray.

"Carl Knight called earlier," she informed him as she arranged cups and spoons.

"What did he want?"

"He just said your Inspector Loman tried to talk to him. He wants to know why."

"Was he out of sorts or upset?"

Rona shook her head. "Not in the least. He was just asking. He even offered Loman to go to Scotland Yard tomorrow morning, at ten o'clock, I think."

"All's well, then," Houston said. "I just hope you didn't tell him about the manuscript and all that..."

Rona looked at him in amazement. "Oh yes, you asked me about a typewritten manuscript of his and I gave it to you. What was that all about?"

"Let's not go into that now," Houston said. "Let's have our coffee first."

Rona laughed and filled the cups. Mike Houston reached for a newspaper. But soon he caught himself staring at the letters without reading any further. His thoughts were already back on Mrs Spedro. What was the name of the book she had written - 'Economics Today' or something like that? He dropped the newspaper, his gaze skimming the colourful spines of books on the shelf against the living room wall. Most of the books belonged to Rona. He couldn't spot the title he was looking for. If the book was still in the house, it was most likely in Dennis's room.

Houston put down his coffee cup and walked out of the room. Rona glanced after him. She wondered what he was doing, but didn't ask the question.

One wall was occupied by three bookshelves. Houston quickly inspected them. He found three business textbooks. Mrs Spedro's was not among them. Maybe it was in the desk? Houston pulled open the drawers one by one. And finally he found what he was looking for.

It was a large volume. He opened the book.

On the leaf in front of the title page was a dedication. "To Dennis – from Margaretta Spedro."

Houston continued to turn the pages. Words and sentences whose meaning he didn't understand slid past his eyes. And then...

"What's this?" muttered Houston, though he was alone.

He had looked through about a quarter of the thick book when he discovered a square about six inches long had been cut out of the middle of each page. The resulting hole was about two inches deep. If you closed the book, you had a pocket in which you could hide a small object. He wondered if Mrs Spedro, who had given Dennis the book, knew about this. The strange little hole was empty.

Houston heard his daughter call out, returned to the living room and showed her the book.

"How strange, Dad. I've never seen this book before. Dennis didn't tell me about it either."

Houston usually smoked a cigarette with his coffee. He reached into his jacket pocket, but it was empty. He remembered that he'd bought a fresh pack that day and went into the hall to look in his coat.

He pulled the packet out of his coat pocket. A small piece of paper fell out and fluttered to the floor. Houston picked it up. It was half a sheet of typewritten paper with a torn edge. Houston saw that the paper was written on and held it closer to the light. He read: "Kelford has disregarded our instructions against informing the police. The appointment is therefore null and void."

Beneath the two sentences, instead of a signature, was a drawing of a small yellow windmill.

Chapter Six

Inspector Mike Houston stared at the note in his hand. The yellow windmill – there it was again. The little drawing of a funny toy – and yet a symbol of crime. A whole series of crimes...

Despondency gripped Houston. More and more crimes were being committed under the sign of the yellow windmill. But where was the trace that led to the criminal or criminals?

"Where are you, Dad?" shouted Rona from the living room. "Your coffee's getting cold!"

With the note in his hand, he returned to the room. "There, look at that! I went to get the cigarettes out of my coat, and I found this in my pocket."

Rona read it. "But that's... How could the note have got into your coat?"

Houston dropped heavily into his usual armchair. "That's what I'm wondering."

"Did you take it off somewhere and hang it up?" Rona looked at him thoughtfully. "Yes, of course..." she began to answer her own question. "In..."

Houston nodded. "That's right. At Danilo's restaurant, where we met for dinner."

Suddenly he remembered that Bob Harridge had come from the direction of the cloakroom when they had almost collided with one another. "It might have been Bob Harridge," he said slowly, explaining the connection to his daughter.

"Bob?" asked Rona in surprise. "Maybe he had the opportunity but what would he have to do with it? And he wasn't the only person who might have done it. You told me you met Mrs Spedro after you went to Kelford's, and she walked along beside you. Couldn't it be that she..."

"That's true," he had to admit. "She's also a possibility. And maybe there are a few other possibilities. I'll have to think about it."

He took the letter from his pocket that the kidnapper had addressed to Sir Cedric Kelford and compared it with the note from his coat pocket. He was no expert in this field, but that both messages must have been typed on the same typewriter he recognised immediately.

He let Rona in on it. She looked at him seriously. "So that's why you wanted me to give you the manuscript that Carl Knight wrote!"

Houston nodded.

"And was it actually his typewriter?"

Sensing a hope behind her question that he might say no, he lowered his eyes. "I'm afraid there's no doubt about it, Rona."

She jumped up and began to pace restlessly up and down the room. Houston remained silent. Poor child, he thought. She's not just professionally connected to Knight, she's also friendly with him. It must be hitting her hard.

"So what are you going to do?" asked Rona after a while in a stressed voice.

He shrugged his shoulders. "I don't know, love," he said quietly. "That depends entirely on what Knight has to say tomorrow when he visits Scotland Yard."

***

"Bloody hell!" groaned Superintendent Gerald Elder. "Instead of getting anywhere, we keep getting new mysteries thrown at us!" He slapped the flat of his hand on his desk. "Tell me yourself, Houston, and you, Loman – we haven't had a confounded case like this for years, have we?"

Inspector Mike Houston and his colleague Loman were silent. Elder saw Houston's pinched lips.

"I don't blame you, Mike. It's not your fault that we're not getting anywhere," the Superintendent quickly added. "But it's maddening! The note they slipped into your pocket. And then this book you found in your son's room. Hand it over to me again!"

"We have examined it carefully, sir," Loman intervened. "And even the specialists in the laboratory have been unable to find anything."

Elder opened the thick book.

"It's curious, this secret compartment cut into the pages," he muttered.

While the Superintendent looked at the book, humming to himself, Loman turned to his colleague Houston. "Maybe the burglar Rona surprised in Dennis's room was after what this secret compartment contained," he surmised.

"I suppose so," Houston said.

The Superintendent looked up. "If only we knew what was in that book! I have a feeling that would put us on the right track. But alas..."

Resignedly, he pushed the book aside and reached for the slip of paper containing the kidnapper's latest communication.

"So what do we do about this ransom situation, sir?" inquired Houston. "Sir Cedric Kelford was supposed to deposit the money in a telephone box in Haydock Green. But in this note," he pointed to the paper, "the kidnapper now states that the appointment is void because Sir Cedric has notified the police."

"I know, I know." Elder's voice sounded irritated. "But it could also be that this note didn't come from the kidnappers at all. That's unlikely – but what is certain in this damned job? In any case, we can't afford to ignore even the slightest chance. It stays the same way as before – Sir Cedric is to go there and deposit the money, and we, we'll have the perimeter of the green staked out as planned."

Loman looked doubtfully at his superior. "But if the message isn't from the kidnappers, who is it from...?"

The ringing of the phone interrupted him. Elder picked it up. The sergeant in the lobby reported that Sir Cedric Kelford wished to speak to the Superintendent urgently.

A few minutes later the office door was flung open and Kelford rushed in. "It's all over now!" he exclaimed excitedly. "Somebody here mustn't have kept their mouth shut!"

He threw a note on the table. The three detectives bent over it. It was a duplicate of the note Houston had found in his coat pocket.

"This came with the morning mail," Kelford said in exasperation. "What am I supposed to do now?"

"First I suggest you sit down and calm yourself, Sir Cedric," said Elder. "Have you got the envelope the note came in?" Sir Cedric fumbled in his pockets and finally found the envelope.

"The postmark is clearly visible," Houston noted. "London W1. But it's hardly going to help us much."

Kelford could hold on no longer. "Do you realise that my child may now be killed by those swine?" he burst out. He buried his face in his hands in despair.

"Are you quite sure, sir, that you haven't spoken to anyone about the ransom letter and our arrangements?" asked Elder after the bank president had calmed down a little.

"I haven't uttered a single word to a single person outside of this building," Kelford insisted. "Something must have leaked from here! And now these thugs won't give me another chance! My child..."

"But sir!" interrupted Elder. "Let's try to look at the whole thing calmly. Excitement will get us nowhere. One thing is certain: the kidnapper or kidnappers want money! Why else would they have kidnapped the child in the first place? This is just a shot in the dark." He pointed to the note. "But you can be sure – you will get a second chance. Believe me, we know from experience."

Kelford pulled out his handkerchief and dried the beads of sweat from his forehead. "Your experience is all very well, but do you really believe, gentlemen, that the kidnapper is behaving as you expect?"

Mike Houston put his hand on Kelford's arm. "They'll try to extract more ransom money from you, you can be sure of that. The only difference being maybe it'll be ten thousand pounds next time!"

Kelford clenched his hands together. "And if it was double that – I'd pay it. What does money mean to me? I care about my child!"

He looked from one to the other. "So you really think Susan – is still alive?" he asked haltingly. "You're not just saying that to reassure me?"

"We're convinced of it," the Superintendent assured him calmly, and Houston and Loman nodded.

Slowly Kelford stood up. "I have to go now. God grant that you're right!"

He took his leave. Houston waited until the door had closed behind him. "I just want to know how the kidnapper found out about Kelford informing us about the ransom note. That the leak's not here with us I could swear. Kelford himself must have talked to somebody about it. It can't be any other way."

"Certainly," Elder confirmed. "It was just striking how adamantly he denied it. The fault lies with him, and he knows it..."

The phone rang again and the sergeant at reception reported that Knight had arrived. "Show him up in a few minutes!"

Elder turned to Houston.

"I don't like this Knight, from what you've told me, Mike. He may be harmless. But you just don't know where you really stand with him. After all, we have to assume that he would be in a position to exert some influence over your daughter Rona."

Houston felt again the feeling of deep perplexity that had never quite left him since the death of his son Dennis. He'd come to realise how little he'd known about his own son. And Rona – what did he really know about her?

"By the way, about Rona, Mike – I've arranged for O'Donovan to take your daughter under his wing. He's one of our best people and he'll look after her properly. She won't notice a thing. I think this is the right thing to do after what happened to your Dennis."

"Thank you very much, sir," Houston said. "She travels a lot and meets a lot of people. It comes with her job. I feel relieved to think that someone is keeping an eye on her."

"So it's agreed!" the Superintendent replied.

There was a knock and Carl Knight entered.

Houston immediately noticed that the young playwright was dressed much more carefully than usual. Instead of his usual battered flannels and a sports jacket, he wore a dark blue suit with a fancy waistcoat. Superintendent Elder immediately got to the heart of the matter. He showed Knight the kidnapper's last communication to Kelford.

Houston watched the author keenly. Knight made no move to take the note in his hand and read the text.

"Now, please look at this!" Elder slid Knight the film script Rona had given her father.

"Yes, I know that one," Knight said quietly. "So what about it?" He looked around the room questioningly.

"Compare the typed letters on the documents, sir, if you will," Elder prompted him.

The three detectives waited until Knight had examined the typing.

"Yes, of course," Knight said flatly. "This is written on my old Mercury typewriter. An excellent and reliable machine. I often wish I'd never sold her."

"You sold her?" repeated Elder in a sharp tone.

"Yes – a few weeks ago. I got a cheque for some foreign rights and so I decided to buy a new typewriter from it."

"Did you sell your Mercury privately?" asked Houston.

"No, I took it to Elcocks in Conway Court, just off Fleet Street. They deal a lot in second-hand typewriters. It shouldn't be a problem to find out where it was sold on to."

He picked up his hat and looked around the room jauntily. "Is that all you wanted to know, gentlemen?" he asked.

Superintendent Elder leaned forward on his desk and looked urgently at Carl Knight with his green eyes. "There are still a great many things we want to know," he replied coolly and deliberately. "The question is, Mr Knight, how much do you want to tell us?"

Knight immediately went into a defensive posture. "What are you getting at exactly?" he asked.

"Among other things, the disappearance of Susan Kelford and the murder of Mary Latimer."

"And what should I know about that?" There was a shade of uncertainty in his voice.

"I'm giving you an opportunity to tell us now, sir" Elder replied unemotionally.

"Are you saying you think I'm involved in these crimes?" said Carl Knight in a demanding tone. "Remember, you are speaking before two witnesses here."

"What I'm saying is that you would make it a lot easier on yourself if you told us what you know instead of letting us find out. Because if we do find out something, it could be a lot more unpleasant for you."

"I don't like your tone or your demeanour, Superintendent," Knight said. "If you want something more from me, you know where to find me," he said and left.

Elder looked at his two colleagues. "What do you make of that?"

Houston shrugged.

"I don't know. His indignation sounded genuine. However – did you see how pale he suddenly became? But that could have been a result of his anger."

Loman nodded. "Not that I want to criticise you, sir – but perhaps you were a bit harsh."

Elder raised his hands in resignation and dropped them on the desk. "You may be right. Well, let's get on with it!"

***

Houston returned to his own office and called Dr Spedro. The doctor seemed very surprised when Houston demanded to speak to his wife.

"I'm sorry, Inspector, but she has gone to the country to visit friends. Is there anything I can do to help?"

"I'm afraid not, Doctor. The matter can wait until your wife returns. But I do have one more question, though. You told me that Mary Latimer became acquainted with you through Sir Cedric Kelford."

"Yes, that's right, Inspector. She came to me on Sir Cedric's recommendation."

Houston had to struggle not to let any sharpness come into his tone as he continued. "Then what do you make of the following, Doctor: Sir Cedric says he'd never heard of the girl until he read her name in the papers yesterday..."

Spedro interrupted him. He spoke faster than usual, and his foreign accent came through more strongly. "I'm most reluctant to contradict Sir Cedric, Inspector. Perhaps I was mistaken. I have so many patients, you know, sometimes it's hard to know where your head is. If Sir Cedric says so... As I was saying – I may well have been mistaken."

"All right," Houston grumbled. It seemed to him that the doctor was making excuses. "I don't think I need to remind you, Doctor, that this is a murder inquiry. The more I find out about the dead girl, the greater the prospect is of finding her killer."

"Of course, Inspector. When my wife returns, I will ask her to get in touch with you, as you seem to think it is very important."

"It is very important," Houston said emphatically and, satisfied, he hung up the phone and told Loman he was going home for lunch.

It was quite late when he arrived and Rona had already eaten. She was standing in the hallway in front of the mirror getting ready to go out.

Houston avoided bringing the conversation immediately to Carl Knight's visit to Scotland Yard, and his daughter didn't ask any questions. He watched as she carefully put on her scarf.

"I've got some shopping to do," she chatted. "And tonight I'm going to the theatre with a friend. We're going to see a play in the West End."

The thought flashed through Houston's mind that Sergeant O'Donovan, Rona's "guardian angel", would have a very full schedule for the afternoons and evenings, of which he was not yet aware.

"And what are you doing?" she asked.

"Routine stuff. By the way..."

She turned to him. "Yes?"

"Do you happen to remember when Carl Knight gave you that film script?"

Rona thought for a moment before answering, "It'll have been about six months ago." She hesitated. "Did you ask him about it?"

Houston shook his head. "Not directly. He said he sold his typewriter a few weeks ago. I'll check it out, but I'm sure he was telling the truth. Now, don't let me stop you, Rona. After the excitement of the last few weeks, something like a night out with a friend will do you good."

After she left the flat, Houston went to the window and watched her walk down the street. A stocky man in his middle years crossed the road and followed Rona at a distance of thirty yards. O'Donovan can be counted on, Houston thought.

***

After lunch, Houston left the house and walked quickly to the nearest underground station. At the newspaper stand he stopped and bought an evening paper.

A man with a suitcase came around the corner of the newsstand and almost collided with him. Slowly, Houston walked down the stairs. There were few travellers at this time of day and the platform was almost deserted. Houston wandered restlessly up and down. When a distant rumble from the tunnel announced the arrival of the train, he stepped to the edge of the platform.

Suddenly he heard a murderous scream behind him. A group of schoolboys with gym bags came hurtling down the stairs. Houston turned back to the tracks and faced the train as it shot straight out of the dark tube tunnel.

Then a violent blow hit his back. The force almost knocked him off his feet. Houston struggled to regain his balance. He was breathing heavily.

"Thank you very much," he called out to the man in the blue overalls who had saved him. "Wait a minute!" Quickly he looked around. It must have been a suitcase, he thought. Someone threw a suitcase into my back so that I should fall onto the tracks in front of the incoming train! He glanced up the stairs but there were only a few women and a little girl standing there.

"You've been lucky, my friend," the man in the blue overalls addressed him. "Can't imagine a worse way to die."

"Did you see it happen?" asked Houston.

The other raised his shoulders. "Not exactly I didn't. But that suitcase there," he pointed behind Houston, who immediately wheeled around, "it came whizzing in from above. Sailed right past my right ear. You know the rest."

Houston bent down to the suitcase. It was made of cheap material. It had burst on impact. Houston opened the locks and lifted the lid. The suitcase contained two heavy iron weights. Nothing else.

Houston examined the case but found no clue to its origin.

He straightened up. The man in the overalls asked, "What are we going to do with this thing?"

"I'll take care of it," Houston said. "I'll take it with me."

By now a small crowd had formed around the two men. The train was still stopping.

Houston and the other man got on and sat down next to each other. The Inspector put the suitcase down and pulled out his notebook.

"If you will kindly give me your name and address..."

The man in overalls fended off Houston's repeated words of thanks.

"Well, listen," he grinned. "What else was I supposed to do, standing there? But tell me – you are going to the police, aren't you, mate?"

Houston smiled. "I'm already on my way, right there. To Scotland Yard."

He pulled out his pipe, stuffed it and lit it. The smoke calmed him. He began to think quietly about the incident. Someone was watching him, that was certain. After that murder attempt on the platform, he was no longer so sure that those shots in the darkness had been meant for Bob Harridge. He would have to be very careful from now on and be constantly on the alert for an attack.

Houston deposited the case at Scotland Yard and went straight on to the 'Rising Sun' in Cheapside, the place Bob Harridge had told him about. Bob had picked up that Mary Latimer had apparently been a regular there.

"Well," said the landlord, "regular is a bit of an exaggeration. But she came in from time to time. And she caught my eye, Inspector. Not exactly the sort of girl we usually have here. Different somehow, you know?"

"Did she come alone?"

The landlord pondered. "She seemed to be meeting a young man here. Anyway, I've seen her with one a couple of times. Some student type, you know, messy dark hair, black horn-rimmed glasses. You want me to try to find out who he is? I can try. If he comes back, I'll let you know."

Houston's next destination was the typewriter shop Carl Knight had indicated near Fleet Street. As the Inspector had expected, it turned out that the writer's information was correct.

"But I'm afraid we no longer have that machine," the dealer said. "Mr A. P. Arnold, number 29, Ainsworth Court in Bloomsbury is the purchaser."

"Do you remember him? What was he like?"

The old man frowned. "He was quite a young man, I seem to remember. Horn-rimmed glasses, black, if I'm not mistaken. His hair fell onto his forehead when he was trying out the machine. That's all I can tell you, I'm afraid."

Houston wrote down the address and left the shop. Is it possible that the young man Mary Latimer met in that pub is the same as the typewriter buyer? he asked himself as he drove to Bloomsbury.

Flat No. 29 Ainsworth Court was on the first floor of a huge block of flats. Houston pressed the bell button. Inside, a bell chimed. He heard radio music, but no one answered. He rang the bell twice more, then looked around cautiously. There was no one to be seen.

He pushed hard against the door. It gave way and swung open. He quickly scurried inside and quietly let the door slide shut behind him.

He knocked on the door of the room that had the radio.

There was no answer.

He pushed down the handle, opened the door a crack and pushed his head through. There was a bed against the opposite wall. The quilt had slipped down and lay half on the floor. He raised his eyes to the figure in the bed. She didn't move. With two or three movements he was beside her. He glanced at her face.

He recognised her immediately. Someone had strangled her. With a scarf. Houston paled when he saw the pattern. It was his daughter Rona's scarf.

Chapter Seven

The silk scarf was around the woman's neck like a shimmering snake. Someone had thrown it over her head from behind and pulled it tight.

Inspector Mike Houston breathed laboriously. He bent over the bed and began to untie the scarf from the lifeless body. He held it so that more light fell on it.

There was no doubt about it. The colour, the pattern, the small tear in one corner close to the hem, the scent – Rona's perfume. It was his daughter's scarf all right.

With trembling fingers he stuffed the scarf into his coat pocket. His hands trembled as he took the woman's arm hanging down to the floor, feeling for the place where he should have felt her pulse. He knew beforehand that it would be in vain. Margaretta Spedro was dead.

Houston dropped the arm and stood up heavily.

Unbelievably, Rona.... What was she supposed to have to do with this woman's death? And yet – it was her scarf. He had seen it on her that very afternoon when she had been standing in front of the mirror getting ready to go out. Was there a connection between his family and this series of crimes? His son Dennis had been murdered. And now Rona's scarf used as a murder weapon ...

Houston walked heavily into the next room. It was the living room. The telephone was on a small table next to an old-fashioned writing desk, closed with a roller blind.

Houston called the nearest police station and asked to notify his colleague Loman in Scotland Yard. He hung up and pushed up the wooden blind. It revealed a typewriter. Houston looked at it. It was a Mercury. This discovery didn't surprise the Inspector. He'd got the address of this flat from the dealer who sold second-hand machines. And this had to be the machine he was looking for. What he did now was routine. He put in a sheet of paper and typed a few lines. He read what he had written. And he was immediately convinced: this was the machine that Carl Knight had sold to the Elcocks company.

Before a sergeant from the nearest police station arrived, Houston had already searched the entire flat. He found nothing else to arouse suspicion.

"Wait here until I come back," he instructed the sergeant. "Leave everything like that, including the body."

Quickly he left the house and went to the police car parked outside. He gave the driver his address. "Drive as fast as you can!"

He was turning the key in the front door lock when he noticed the shadow of a male figure nearby. "Is that you, O'Donovan?"

"Yes, sir." Sergeant O'Donovan approached. Houston pulled the key out of the lock again. "Get into the car with me for a minute. I need to ask you something."

Silently they got in and settled into the back seats. "Did you lose Rona's trail?" asked Houston.

Rona's guard shook his head. "No, sir. Your daughter's there. In the house, I mean."

"But she was going to the theatre."

"That may be," O'Donovan said, "but she didn't go anywhere near a theatre whilst I've been tailing her. After her shopping spree this afternoon, I followed her to a flat in Cromwell Road."

Carl Knight's flat, Houston supposed.

"She stayed there for about an hour," the sergeant continued. "At around seven o'clock she was back here. And since then..."

Houston looked sharply at O'Donovan.

"And you're sure she hasn't gone anywhere else, even for five minutes?"

"I should have noticed, sir," O'Donovan assured him, "I followed her everywhere."

Houston thought quickly.

"How long are you on duty today?"

"Until eleven, sir, unless you wish me to stay on longer."

Houston opened the car door. "You'll know soon enough," he said as he got out. Quickly he went into the house.

Rona was squatting in an armchair in the living room, had her legs pulled under her and was reading a script book.

"I thought you wanted to go to the theatre," Houston said abruptly. It sounded almost reproachful.

Rona looked up in surprise. "When I got back from shopping, Carl called. He said he needed to speak to me urgently, right away. I didn't know how long it would take. So I called my girlfriend and cancelled."

"Was it really that important?"

"Of course. It was about the play."

"I see – about the play," Houston murmured.

Rona frowned. "Yes, Ambrose Wyler – you know, that theatre entrepreneur – wants to put it on. He wants some changes made, of course. That was the reason Carl called me and wanted to talk to me."

"How long were you with him?"

"Maybe an hour. He had a lot of new ideas and..."

Houston interrupted her. "What about the scarf you were wearing the last time I saw you this afternoon? Were you wearing it when you visited Carl Knight at his flat?"

Confused, she looked at him. "Yes, I think I was. By the way – now that you mention it, it occurs to me: I think I left it there. Anyway, on the way home I suddenly realised that I hadn't got it on. Yes, I must have left it with him. I wouldn't know where else... Yes, I remember now: I put it over the little bust of Nero that stands in Carl's hall."

"That's strange," Houston said.

"What's odd about it?" asked Rona. She jumped out of the chair. "He walked me into the hallway, helped me into my coat, we talked non-stop about the changes we planned to make in the play. We were so engrossed in conversation, you see. That's when I just forgot about the thing, and he didn't pay attention to it either. Has nothing like that ever happened to you before?"

"All right, all right, Rona." He reached into his pocket and pulled out the scarf. "Is it this one?"

She glanced at it and nodded. "Yes, of course. That's it." She lifted her head. "Did you go to Carl's?"

"No," Houston replied, shoving the scarf back into his pocket. He took a deep breath. "I'll explain everything later."

He turned to the door. Hand on the handle, he turned to her once more. "Don't go out of the house again, Rona. And when I'm out, put the security chain on and see to it that all the windows are closed."

"But, Dad..."

"I can't tell you any more now, love. I've got to go. I've work to do."

Before she could ask anything else, he was gone.

***

Houston gave O'Donovan some instructions concerning Rona and had the police van take him to Dr Spedro's nursing home. The receptionist asked him to wait. "Dr Spedro is making his evening rounds, I'm afraid. He gets very displeased if he's disturbed."

"But it's urgent," Houston insisted. "I must see him at once. Right away, do you understand?"

She disappeared to fetch the doctor. But five minutes passed before Spedro appeared.

"I'm sorry, Inspector, but I really can't tell you anything about Mary Latimer until my wife returns. I've already told you that..."

Houston shook his head. "She's not coming back, Doctor," he said slowly.

"What do you mean?" asked Spedro fiercely.

Houston looked at him fixedly. "I'm afraid I have some bad news for you, Doctor. Your wife has been found dead."

Dr Spedro turned pale. "But that's impossible, Inspector! My wife has gone to the country, to stay with friends. I don't see why..."

"We'd best go to your consulting room," Houston said. "We'd better not talk about it here in the corridor."

"Yes, come along," Spedro said tonelessly and preceded Houston.

The Inspector closed the door. "She was in a flat in Ainsworth Court in Bloomsbury," he said quietly. "Dead. I found her myself. It's her, Spedro, there's no doubt about it. I'm sorry for you – but my job sometimes requires me to deliver such news. The best thing is for you to come there with me."

Spedro nodded silently and stepped up to a shelf, took out a brandy bottle and poured a glass full. He emptied it in one go.

He turned the glass in his hand. "Ainsworth Court – I've never heard of it, Inspector."

"You have no acquaintances there?"

"No. – My God, Margaretta..."

Houston was silent for a few moments before he continued. "The flat belongs to an A. P. Arnold. Does that name mean anything to you, Doctor?"

Spedro replied in the negative. "Not that I know of. My wife – there... Of course, she knew a lot of people –

professors, publishing merchants, journalists and such. But I never heard her mention anyone named Arnold."

Houston put his hand on Spedro's arm. "I don't want to push you, Doctor, but I have to. If you feel able to accompany me there now..."

Spedro nodded and followed him.

***

At the flat in Ainsworth Court they found only the sergeant and a second policeman talking to each other.

"It's her," Spedro muttered after glancing at the body. "It's her." He turned away. His face twitched. "Strangled," he muttered. Suddenly he wheeled around. "Who did this, Inspector? Who brought her here? Who did this to her?" he groaned.

"That's what I'm trying to find out," Houston replied. "And I mean, Doctor, now would be the time to tell me everything you know."

Dr Spedro wrung his hands. "But I don't know anything about all this! What could I possibly tell you?"

Houston didn't let up. "There are a lot of unanswered questions in connection with Mary Latimer's death. And there's the fact that your wife was acquainted with my son Dennis, who was also murdered."

Spedro's dark complexion grew even darker. "But I don't know anything! How many times do you want me to repeat that? What could any of it have to do with my wife?"

"I'm here to ask the questions, not answer them," Houston said calmly. "Surely you know that your wife has published a book on economics."

"Of course I know that, Inspector."

"Do you also know that she gave a copy of it to my son Dennis, even with a dedication?"

"I believe she gave several of her students..."

95

Houston nodded. "That's as may be. But in my son's copy we found a small pocket cut into the pages. Apparently this pocket contained a small object. Do you have any idea what that object might have been?"

Spedro stared at him in amazement. "Of course I don't. You're wasting your time, Inspector. You should be out looking for my wife's murderer."

Houston gave him a sharp look. "I know best what to do, doctor. And I warn you, if you're not a little more open with us, you could find yourself in serious trouble."

The doctor's blood rushed to his face. "I don't know what you're talking about. You know that I have a very responsible job, that I am a respected man. And you – you talk to me as if I'm a criminal!"

Houston was about to reply when there was a knock and the sergeant entered. "The forensics people have been examining Mrs Spedro's handbag. Among other things, they found this."

He handed the Inspector a small silver penknife with a cigar cutter worked into one end. Houston examined it carefully. The knife was engraved with initials. Houston read: "C. K."

"It's a somewhat unusual kind of knife – in a woman's handbag," the sergeant commented.

Houston looked up. "Yes, it's fine. Now leave us alone again please, Sergeant."

He waited until the police officer had left the room and held up the knife. "The man is right, doctor. Have you ever seen this knife in your wife's possession?"

Spedro twirled the knife between his fingers. "I think it belongs to Sir Cedric Kelford," he said long-sufferingly.

Houston looked at him in surprise. "Yes, of course. It might be. Those initials – C. K. You may be right – Cedric

Kelford. Yes, I think that will be all for now, Doctor," Houston said.

He went out and gave the sergeant some more instructions. "And when this Mr Arnold arrives, who owns this flat, call me at my home immediately."

As they took the doctor to his flat in the police car, Houston asked him a series of questions, but Dr Spedro insisted he knew nothing more about Mary Latimer. He'd never seen Carl Knight and never heard of Dennis Houston until his death. And he hardly knew anything about his wife's acquaintanceship with Kelford.

"She certainly saw him once when he came to consult me. Maybe she met him again elsewhere – I told you, she knew a lot of people. But I – I don't know anything."

Houston looked after Spedro as he walked with heavy steps to the door of his house.

"Where to now, sir?" the police driver asked. Houston told him Carl Knight's address.

***

The writer opened the door as soon as Houston rang the bell. His amazement at seeing Houston lasted only a second. Then he greeted the Inspector with his usual nonchalance. "Hello, come in! Did you find out anything about my old typewriter?"

"I'm still working on it," Houston said guardedly. "What I'm interested in right now is something else entirely – Rona's scarf."

Knight stared at him. "Rona's scarf? That's what you've come for? What the hell does Rona's scarf have to do with anything?"

Houston didn't answer the question. "She was wearing a scarf when she came here this afternoon, wasn't she?"

Knight nodded. "I think so, yes. Somehow I seemed to notice it."

"Didn't she leave it here?" asked Houston.

97

"I don't know about that, Inspector. But we can have a look."

"She told me she left it in the hallway," Houston continued.

Carl Knight led the way into the hall. They looked behind the table on which stood the Nero's head. This was the only possible place where the scarf could have been mislaid. Houston didn't tell Knight that the scarf was at present in his pocket. He was waiting to see if the author would make even the tiniest slip.

"What's all this about anyway?" asked Knight.

"A woman has been found strangled with a scarf exactly like Rona's," said Houston bluntly. "It probably happened around the time Rona was here, or just after."

"Good Lord! You're not suggesting that Rona –"

"I'm suggesting that someone used Rona's scarf to throw suspicion on her."

Carl stepped back a pace and leaned against the wall. He seemed to have turned pale, and there was a note of apprehension in his voice. "Hadn't you better tell me the name of this woman?"

"She was a Mrs Spedro. Do you know her?"

There was a pause, then Carl Knight said slowly: "The name means nothing to me."

It was obvious that Houston wouldn't gain any further information, so he left and picked up a taxi in the Cromwell Road. As they drove through the deserted streets, he surveyed the day's events. It had been a stroke of inspiration on the part of Superintendent Elder to have Rona kept under observation. She had an alibi as far as the death of Mrs Spedro was concerned; that was the main thing.

It was after midnight when he got home, but he found Rona sitting by the radio. "I kept some coffee for you," she said, and he followed her into the kitchen. "Did you discover anything about my scarf?" she demanded anxiously, as he sat stirring his coffee.

He shook his head and told her of his visit to Carl Knight's flat. "I'm certain I left it there," she said. "Just as I was taking it off, Carl was called to the telephone."

"Why didn't you look for it as you came out?"

"I don't quite know. Maybe I did, sort of subconsciously. I'm sure if it had been where I left it I would have seen it and put it on again. It simply couldn't have been there."

"Then presumably somebody took it. Was there anyone else in the flat?"

"I didn't see anyone. We seemed to be alone all the time." She hesitated a moment, then asked: "You don't think Carl is mixed up in this murder, do you?"

"There's no proof of it. But your scarf will have to be produced in evidence, and you'll be called on to identify it."

Their speculations were cut short by the telephone ringing. Thinking it was the sergeant reporting the return of the mysterious Mr Arnold, Houston lifted the receiver. A soft, pleasant voice said: "Inspector Houston? I thought you'd like to know that Sir Cedric Kelford has had another note about his daughter. This time the demand is for ten thousand pounds. The money is to be taken to Leach's Farm near Petworth tomorrow night. Of course, he won't tell the police this time, but I thought you'd like to know, Inspector."

The line went dead. Houston had the call traced at once, but it had come from a public call box in Hammersmith.

Houston left immediately to visit Sir Cedric. He had to know what Kelford had to say about this latest development.

"Come in, Inspector."

"I'm sorry to trouble you again, sir, but I was wondering if there was anything new you had to report, Sir Cedric?" asked Houston without particular emphasis. Perhaps Sir Cedric would talk about the latest ransom note after all.

The bank president pointedly glanced at his watch. "There's nothing, I'm afraid, Inspector," he said quickly. "And I'm afraid I must ask you to excuse me. I have a great deal to do. A very important visitor has been waiting for ten minutes so if you wouldn't mind ..."

So Kelford had decided not to tell the police about the latest ransom letter and this time to play a lone game.

***

Houston returned to Scotland Yard. Kelford's behaviour had convinced him that Sir Cedric had received a new letter from the blackmailer and that this time he was determined to leave the police out of it and pay the sum demanded.

Loman awaited Houston with the results of his research into the Leach farm.

"Actually, it's not really a farm. More like a little country place with a shack on it. Belongs to a guy named Len Milford. Colleagues say the whole thing is a pretty rotten affair. Milford's let the place go to seed. Seems a bit work-shy. Still, he's always got money. They've suspected him of crookedness for a long time. But they haven't been able to prove anything yet. They'll send a couple of plainclothes men. They'll keep a low profile on the farm until we can get there."

***

Houston's colleague from the county police had some policemen stationed near the Leachs' farm at nightfall. He gave him and Loman directions to the lonely homestead.

"I wish you good luck, Houston. Too bad I can't go with you. But I still have to do my duty here for another hour. Well, you know how it is. Hopefully we can prove something against this Milford guy this time. I haven't liked the guy for a long time."

They drove through Petworth. Two miles past the end of town, Houston ordered the driver to stop. "Turn right here, down the narrow road. And turn off your headlights!"

100

The driver obeyed. Slowly the car turned in the indicated direction.

"The road's fine, sir," the driver muttered. "Seems to be one of the better dirt roads." Straining, he bored his eyes into the darkness.

The car rumbled slowly over the rough road. For a few seconds the pale moon emerged from behind the heavy clouds and the men saw the house.

"Stop here. When we get out, go behind the bushes over there and wait until we come back. And as I said – no lights!" Houston urged the driver.

He and Loman left the car and walked towards the small farmhouse. It was about fifty yards from the potholed road. They saw a faint glow of light behind the window to the right of the front door.

Houston and Loman made the rounds to four strategic points where the county policemen were posted to watch anyone approaching the house. Then they crept on. In a small-fenced paddock opposite the house, they found a hayloft. An ideal hiding place from which they could keep a close eye on the entrance.

Somewhere at the back of the house a dog was barking. If someone approached the back door, they would probably attract the attention of the dog, which would then bark persistently. Houston therefore found it unnecessary to guard the rear entrance as carefully as the front door.

He shivered in the cold night wind.

Loman also turned up his collar and buried his hands deeper in his coat pockets. They listened into the darkness. The dog was silent: nothing stirred outside the farm. Every now and then Houston glanced at the luminous dial of his watch.

They waited for more than an hour. Suddenly they heard the sound of an engine. A car was approaching. They saw no light. Their eyes had become accustomed to the darkness by now. The shadowy car stopped for a moment where a grassy driveway to the house branched off from the bumpy road. Slowly the car started moving again, rolling towards the low building. The dog on the other side began to bark wildly. Almost at the same moment the car stopped, the outside door opened and a man jumped out. He pulled something out of the car. It could have been a large suitcase.

"That must be Kelford," Loman whispered. But they couldn't make out the visitor's face. The man knocked on the front door. A few seconds later, the light from the window next to the door disappeared. The arrival knocked again and immediately the door was opened. The man who appeared in the doorway held a paraffin lamp in his hand. It illuminated his face. Houston had to suppress an exclamation and grabbed Loman by the arm. The two men at the door greeted each other briefly and went inside. The door slammed shut.

"Do you know the man with the lamp?" asked Loman quietly.

"You bet I recognised him," Houston whispered back grimly.

Chapter Eight

The moon had disappeared behind the clouds. Houston and Loman could barely make out the outline of the lonely farmhouse.

"The man with the paraffin lamp," Houston whispered, "that's the fellow who tried to kill me at the Underground station."

"Well, we'll get that boy," Loman hissed.

"I think we'll get started now," Houston agreed. He glanced at the luminous dial on his wristwatch. Three minutes had passed since the arrival of the visitor they thought was Sir Cedric Kelford.

The two Inspectors left their hiding place behind the hayloft. Loman took a small signal whistle from his pocket and gave a short blast. This was the signal for the policemen scattered around the area to approach the farm. Quietly, Houston and Loman approached the door. When they were only a few yards from the entrance, they heard voices from inside the house. They stopped. Loman tapped Houston on the arm and pointed to the window. It was open a crack.

"And I'm telling you – I don't know anything about a little girl." The voice of the man who was probably Len Milford sounded low and rough.

"You must be taking me for a fool," came Sir Cedric Kelford's voice. "You must be..."

The other interrupted him. "All I know is that I was to receive a suitcase containing ten thousand pounds."

Houston signalled to Loman. They ran to the door. Loman whistled a second signal. The door was unlocked, they wrenched it open and rushed through a stone-tiled hall. Seconds later they were face to face with Sir Cedric Kelford and Len Milford.

The farmer tried to reach the door at the other end of the room with a leap.

Loman was quicker. He threw himself in Milford's path and pushed him back. "Stay here, my friend!" he gasped. "And don't make any fuss. The house is surrounded by our people."

Sir Cedric Kelford hadn't uttered a word in surprise. He stood before the fireplace built of rough stone and pressed his hand to his heart.

"Are you all right, sir?" asked Houston.

Kelford nodded wordlessly.

The farmer squirmed under Loman's hard grip. "Who the hell do you think you are to just break into a private house like this?" he roared.

"You know exactly who we are, Mr Milford," Houston snapped at him. "At least, who I am. You remember me, don't you? Have you already forgotten how you hurled that suitcase at me in the Underground station?"

"Get out of here!" said Milford roughly. "I don't know what you're talking about. You're crazy, man!"

"We're leaving right now," Loman assured him. "But you're coming with us."

"You can save yourself the trouble," the farmer growled hatefully. "You won't get anything out of me."

Kelford had dropped into an armchair.

"So you received a second ransom letter," Houston observed. There was no reproach in his tone.

Without a word, Sir Cedric Kelford pulled a piece of paper from his pocket and held it out to Houston. The letter was typed on the same machine as the other communications from the kidnapper that Houston had seen.

"Have you received any sign of life from Susan?" the Inspector asked.

Kelford shook his head. Houston wheeled around to Milford. "What about you?" he barked. "If you've got that child trapped around here somewhere, say so right now! We'll have the place searched."

"You won't find anyone here," grunted the farmer. But he narrowed his eyes. Ever since Houston had described him as the assassin from the Underground station, there had been a fearful tug in his countenance.

Houston stepped up to the table and reached for the bundle of banknotes. "Let's go," he said, striding to the door.

"Come on, Milford!" Loman nudged the farmer.

"You can't pin anything on me!" the farmer protested again weakly.

"We'll see about that," Houston said from the doorway. "And you, Sir Cedric, should also come with us to the police station. We have some things to sort out."

Kelford had stood up. "All right, Inspector. I'll come behind you in my car."

The two Inspectors took the still muttering Milford in between them and led him to the police car which had by now pulled up at the entrance. Houston gave the officers instructions for the search in front of the house, then they drove off. Sir Cedric Kelford followed them in his large American limousine.

Fifteen minutes later, in a room at the police station, Houston opened the interrogation. "Now, Milford," he began, looking sharply at the farmer. "Now let's get something straight. I can put you on trial for attempted murder. And I have a witness to what happened at the tube station."

Milford was silent. His coarse face twitched. Spasmodically he tried to suppress the rising fear.

"On the other hand," Houston continued, "if you decide to tell us everything you know..."

He broke off, letting the implication with which he had intended to give the farmer hope of a more lenient treatment take effect.

"I've already told you I don't know anything," Milford grumbled weakly.

Houston didn't take his eyes off him. "You won't get away with less than five years in prison. You might even get more. Depends on your criminal record. You do have one, don't you?"

Milford straightened up. The feigned defiance certainly fell from him. His eyes flickered.

Houston noticed that the farmer was suddenly uneasy. He paused. He waited.

"All right," he said after a long silence. "If you prefer to spend years behind bars..."

"No." Milford swallowed. "I'll tell you what I know. But believe me, it's not much. I don't really belong to the gang. I do what I'm told and I don't ask questions. Really, I just work for them from time to time. Like tonight."

"You mean the Yellow Windmill Gang?" interjected Houston.

Milford nodded. "That's right."

"Is it a big organisation?"

The farmer raised his shoulders. "I don't know. But I think so."

Houston looked at him searchingly. "And what's their line of work?"

Milford hesitated a moment before answering. "Blackmail. They gather information on people who have a dark spot in their past. And then... They did the same with me. They found out I did a crooked thing once just after the war..."

Houston raised his hand. "Let's leave that aside, Milford," he interjected to encourage the farmer. "Let's stick to the case

106

we're dealing with today. What do you have to say about it? What instructions did you have for tonight?"

"I was to take the suitcase with the money to Victoria Station and check it in at the left luggage office. After that, I was to send the luggage ticket to this address." As he spoke, he fingered in his shirt pocket and produced a small slip of paper.

"Give it here!" Houston took the note and read: "Mr. A. P. Arnold, 29 Ainsworth Court, London W. C. 1."

The flat where he had found Mrs Spedro strangled! The flat where the typewriter was kept on which the blackmail letters had been written. Mr. A. P. Arnold. He still hadn't returned to his flat since the police had been guarding it. Mr. A. P. Arnold... The dealer who had sold Carl Knight's second-hand typewriter had described the man of that name as a young man with horn-rimmed glasses and untidy black hair. The same description had been given by the landlord of the Rising Sun of the young man with whom the murdered Mary Latimer had met several times in his pub shortly before her death. This A. P. Arnold is a key figure in this mysterious, murderous game, Houston thought. But who's the real person behind the name?

He looked up. "Have you ever seen Arnold before?"

Milford shook his head. "Never."

"And what do you know about Sir Cedric's little daughter?"

"All I had to do was to receive the money," the farmer insisted. "I didn't even know who would bring it here."

Loman intervened. By now he too had read the note with the address. "And you're seriously telling us that you've never met anyone from this organisation in person?"

Milford half turned to him. "Believe me," he said in an imploring tone. "They do everything over the telephone or in writing, through the post. I don't know who's behind it. And
107

someone is always watching me. I'm sure they've someone out at the farm now, keeping a close eye on what's going on. I don't even dare go back there now."

Houston glanced at Loman. Loman nodded briefly. Milford's statement sounded credible. They were obviously dealing with a particularly sophisticated gang. Not even the henchmen who carried out the orders knew who the mastermind was.

"All right, Milford," Houston said. "We can arrange for you to stay here for a few days." He asked the sergeant at the police station to keep Milford in custody.

"We're going back to town now. As you've a lot of money with you," he turned to Sir Cedric Kelford, who had been listening to the interrogation in silence, "I think it better for me to go with you in your car."

The police car followed them. Sir Cedric Kelford sat silently at the wheel. Houston's attempts to start a conversation were met only with a dismissive growl. He gave no answer to the Inspector's questions.

"I wish to God," he said after a long time, "you had stayed out of this affair, Houston. My gut tells me this was the last chance to get Susan back." He pressed his lips tightly together and his cheekbones stood out.

"I can understand your bitterness, Sir Cedric," Houston objected. "But it didn't, in my opinion, look as hopeless as you portray this matter of tonight. Remember – Milford knew nothing at all about Susan."

Sir Cedric shook his head vigorously. "I didn't expect Susan to be at the farm, if that's what you mean. After all, the kidnappers knew I'd gone to the police after receiving the first ransom letter, and they had to consider that I would do it again the second time. Then they would have lost their trump card, the child – and the money too. No, they didn't even think of handing Susan over to me at the farm. But I could probably have picked her up somewhere else, after I had brought them the ten thousand pounds as arranged. I want my child back, Inspector. You want to arrest the culprit. If you had a little more imagination, shadowed this Milford chap on the way to Victoria station, and then waited for the person who was to pick up the suitcase.... That way you might have got close to the kidnapper. But to just barge in like that in the middle of the conversation with Milford – you blew it, Houston."

The Inspector listened calmly to the accusations. "Talking smart after the event is no art, Sir Cedric," he said. "If you had come to us after you'd received the second ransom letter, we could have considered together how best to proceed. We probably would have done exactly what you are now recommending after the fact. But if you don't want to cooperate with us, you'll have to leave it to us to do what we think is right under the circumstances."

Kelford slowly calmed down. "I know you're doing your utmost, Inspector. But when I think of my innocent poor child in the hands of those thugs – it makes me furious."

"I understand that very well, Sir Cedric. But if only you'd finally realise that we are only too anxious to help you!"

Outside his home in Eaton Square, Sir Cedric Kelford said goodbye to Houston. The Inspector watched him walk with heavy steps to the door, depressed and dejected by the failure.

Houston wandered through the night-empty streets to the flat in Ainsworth Court. The awake sergeant reported to him that the mysterious Mr. A. P. Arnold had still not appeared. On the ground floor, Houston sought out the night porter of the apartment block. He was a talkative Irishman. He described the tenant Arnold verbosely. But he knew no more about him than the landlord of the 'Rising Sun' and the typewriter dealer had already told the Inspector.

Houston didn't reach his flat until around six in the morning. He set the alarm clock for nine, lay down and immediately fell asleep.

When he left the bathroom three and a half hours later, Rona was waiting for him. "Breakfast will be ready in a minute."

Quickly Houston got dressed.

"I was very worried about you," Rona welcomed him to the breakfast table. "Where have you been all night? What happened?"

He told her briefly what had occurred. She could tell he was disappointed and quickly changed the subject.

Houston reached for the morning paper. Soon the doorbell rang and Rona ushered Bob Harridge in.

"Well, Bob – what are you doing here, at this hour?" wondered Houston. "Surely you should be at the bank by now."

Bob Harridge looked very smug. "Just goes to show you that the supposedly all-knowing police don't know everything after all," he said with a laugh. "In front of you, you see one of the latest pretenders to the good old private enterprise spirit."

"Are you saying you don't work at the bank any more?" exclaimed Rona.

Bob sat down and took the cup of coffee Rona offered him. "Just that. I've been toying with the idea of going into business for myself for a long time. Now I've finally done it. I've opened a small estate agency in Tooting. I never start before ten o'clock." He smiled. "I thought I'd just pop back in and see how the case is going. Surely there must be some news by now?"

"And what kind of news do you expect?" asked Houston.

"Well, I thought perhaps you'd followed up my tip about Mary Latimer and her visits to the 'Rising Sun'."

"I did, Bob, and I'm very grateful to you for the information. It may even prove very useful in the further course of the manhunt. But now that you're here, perhaps you could help me clarify a few other things."

Bob lit a cigarette. "But of course, sir, if I am able to." He leaned back comfortably in the armchair.

Houston leaned forward. "Have you ever heard of a man called A. P. Arnold?"

"Arnold? I don't think so. I'm sorry I can't help you with that one, Inspector."

"You also never heard Mary Latimer mention anyone of that name?"

"I'm quite sure she never mentioned that name in my presence. Why should she have done so? I told you a few days ago – you'll remember – that I spoke very little to the girl," Bob Harridge replied. "By the way, Inspector, is it true what I read in the paper – that you're also handling this murder case in Ainsworth Court? Wasn't it a Mrs Spedro or something like that?"

Houston nodded. "That's right. Is that who Mary Latimer was talking about?"

Harridge brushed the ash from his cigarette. "No, not that either. It doesn't look as if I can be much use to you after all this morning, sir."

"Have you been involved in any other incidents since that evening you were with us, Bob?" inquired Houston.

Harridge looked at him in surprise. "Why should I? You don't mean to say that the fellow in the car shot at me?"

"He might well have done," Houston replied dryly.

"But – but why?"

"You might have some information that these fellows would like – suppressed."

Harridge's eyes widened in disbelief. "I'm just a lowly bank clerk – or at least I was!"

Houston had to laugh at the sight of him. "That's all right, Bob, forget it." He looked around. Rona had left the room and was out of earshot. "As a matter of fact, I'm pretty sure," he continued more quietly, "that the shots were aimed at me. And what's more, they tried to kill me a second time."

"Good God, you need a bodyguard or something!"

"Occupational hazard, I'm afraid..." smiled Houston.

Shaking his head, Bob Harridge stood up and took his leave. Rona, who had been about to return to the room, accompanied him to the door.

"Shall we go out for dinner one evening to celebrate my escape from the bank?" Bob invited her.

"I'd love to, Bob. But I've got a lot of busy rehearsals over the next few days..."

"You'll get through them, don't worry." He didn't let her objection stand. "So let's say eight o'clock tomorrow night at Danilo's restaurant. Agreed?"

"All right, I'll be there," Rona promised.

***

Houston finished reading the morning paper, then set off. At Scotland Yard, Loman received him with the news that Carl Knight had agreed to have his fingerprints taken.

"Anything new from Ainsworth Court?" asked Houston. "Anything on this A. P. Arnold character?"

"Still no sign of him." Loman accompanied Houston to Superintendent Elder's room. "I've already told him in broad outline what took place at the farm last night. But he still wants to hear your report."

Elder finally came to talk about Sir Cedric Kelford. "I don't know what to make of the man," he confessed. "Even his behaviour last night... He should have notified us when he received the second ransom letter ordering him to leave ten thousand pounds at that lonely farm."

112

Houston agreed with him. "Still, there is an excuse for him. He's desperate. He's worried about his child."

There was a knock and a sergeant entered. He handed the Superintendent a cigarette case.

"It was found in Mrs Spedro's coat pocket, sir," he reported. "We showed it to her husband. He confirms that it was hers. But he doesn't know where she got it."

The Superintendent turned the case over in his hands. It was gold and bore initials in one corner. "Are those the first letters of her name?" asked Elder. "M. S.?" He passed the case to Houston.

"Yes," Houston said. "Margaretta Spedro." He stepped over to the window with the cigarette case and looked at it carefully. Then he slowly returned to the desk.

"Look at the initials again, sir," he prompted his superior. Elder and Loman bent over the case.

"If you look closely," Houston continued, "you will see that the letter S was originally an R. This letter has been subsequently altered. This letter has been subsequently reworked."

"Indeed it has!" Elder glanced at Houston. "You look very pleased with yourself, Houston. What does all this mean, do you think?"

"I find it confirms a certain theory of mine," Houston said. "I'll tell you what it is later. There's no hurry."

***

Rona Houston was admiring Bob Harridge's new suit when they met in the foyer of Danilo's Restaurant, and she told him so. Bob was visibly flattered and murmured that being your own boss gave you a whole new lease of life.

At dinner he spoke in a very confidential tone. "Now that I have left the bank, Rona, I can take the liberty of talking to you about some things that concern me in connection with your brother's death," he began. "That is – whether there is a connection, I don't really know. But it could be the case."

Tensely, Rona looked at him. He filled her wine glass and continued, "Of course, this is all strictly confidential, Rona. A few months ago we had some trouble in the office. It had been discovered that information about big plans of some of our major banking clients had been leaked to their competitors. If it had been just one case, it was possible that the indiscretions had started elsewhere. But it wasn't an isolated case. And so the bank staff came under suspicion, or at least some of us did."

Rona frowned and put down her glass. "Dennis never told me about that."

Harridge looked surprised.

"He didn't hint at anything at all. Oh well, it's understandable that he left it un– What are you saying?"

Bob pressed on. "Well, to be frank – the main suspicion eventually fell on Dennis. The matter was investigated, Dennis was questioned extensively, and I think they kept him under surveillance for a while too. But they found no evidence against him."

Rona bowed her head. "Sir Cedric Kelford never mentioned any of this," she said quietly.

"Why should he, Rona? I explained to you, didn't I, that they didn't find a thing to hold against Dennis?"

She looked up. "And why are you telling me this now?"

Bob noticed how pale Rona had become during his account. "I'm just trying to help," he said, a little offended. "It seems to me that Dennis got mixed up with some quite dangerous people. And when he refused to do what they wanted him to do, he... It could have been like that, Rona."

She nodded silently. It was the most plausible explanation she had yet heard for her brother's death. She resolved to speak to Sir Cedric Kelford about it at the next opportunity.

She put her hand over her glass when Bob Harridge asked if she'd like a refill. "No, thank you. I – I... Don't be angry with me, Bob, but I think it's best if I go home now."

Bob Harridge made no attempt to hold her back.

***

On the way home, Rona thought about what Bob had told her. She was deeply troubled. She looked at her watch and made a decision. She turned the car around and drove back into town.

When she pulled up at Kelford's house in Eaton Square, it was half past ten. Kelford received her immediately.

"Excuse my appearance, Miss Houston." He pointed down at himself to his house jacket and slippers. "But of course I didn't expect to have such a nice visitor as yourself just now."

He took her by the hand and escorted her to a rocking chair in front of the fireplace. "Well, what brings you to me?" He offered her a cigarette and gave her a light. "Would you like something to drink?"

Rona decided on whisky. She waited to answer his question until he too had taken a seat.

"It's about my brother," she began quietly. "I've heard that he's been suspected of leaking bank secrets." She didn't mention from whom she'd heard it.

Sir Cedric rubbed his chin thoughtfully. "It's true," he admitted hesitantly. "It was an unpleasant story, and your brother was under suspicion for a time. I had the whole matter very thoroughly investigated. It was not at all easy. But I can tell you, we didn't find the slightest clue to conclude that your brother was involved in the affair."

Rona listened in silence. He saw that she was still brooding. He stood up and began pacing back and forth in the room.

"We haven't let the matter rest, of course," Sir Cedric continued. "We can't, if only because of our bank clients. Our suspicions go in an entirely different direction. We hope to find the solution to the mystery soon. It is expected daily that the case will be finally solved."

She looked up at him. "And you are quite sure that Dennis wasn't..."

He patted her shoulder gently, reassuringly. "Absolutely certain. You see, we have every reason to assume..."

The ringing of the phone interrupted him. He excused himself to Rona and strode across the wide room to the small table where the phone stood. He lifted the receiver to his ear. Suddenly he let out a strangled scream.

Rona jumped up and took a few steps towards him.

"Susan," he cried in a trembling voice, "Susan, my darling! Is it really you?"

He listened. Rona felt tears welling in her eyes.

Then his tone changed. Apparently someone else was now speaking on the other end of the line. Rona vaguely heard a man's voice.

"Yes, the suitcase is still here," Sir Cedric said. His voice sounded almost impassive.

He's scared, Rona thought. What must he have been through that he, such a powerful man, would talk to a sleazy kidnapper in this way.

"Yes, and the money's in there too," Kelford said. "In small notes, just like you asked for it. All right. Yes, I understand."

He replaced the receiver and stared at the machine. Slowly he raised his eyes and looked at Rona. Beads of sweat stood out on his forehead. His hand shook as he pulled a handkerchief from his breast pocket and dabbed his forehead.

"Miss Houston," he groaned desperately. "You have to help me!"

He breathed laboriously. Rona grabbed him anxiously by the arm. "Are you unwell, Sir Cedric?"

"It will be over in a moment," he replied, forcing himself to calm down. He stepped to a wall shelf, shook a tablet from a small green glass bottle and brought his hand to his mouth. He poured a glass full of water and emptied it half in one go. Slowly he came back to Rona.

"Susan is alive!" he said, visibly calmer now. "I heard her voice. The man said I'd get Susan back immediately if I made sure he got the ten thousand pounds right away."

"And you agreed to that." It was more a statement than a question.

"Of course," said Sir Cedric Kelford. "But that's not all." He looked pleadingly at Rona. "They know you're here with me. And they demand that you hand over the money..."

Rona opened her mouth. She couldn't make a sound. She felt an ice-cold wave wash over her.

Chapter Nine

Rona Houston felt the blood pounding in her temples. She closed her eyes. She wondered how she could still think straight: I'm supposed to hand over the money to the kidnappers! If only it weren't for the fear, my God, that terrible fear!

"They demand that you take the money to Wimbledon Common," Sir Cedric Kelford repeated. He stood close to her, his face close to hers, and she felt the hasty puffs of his breath.

"Shouldn't we call my father?" she asked weakly.

"No, we mustn't take any chances!" cried Kelford. He couldn't suppress the desperation in his voice. "Maybe they've tapped my phone. These people are capable of anything."

With trembling hands, he grabbed her by both shoulders. "Please, Miss Houston, you have to help me! You can't let anything happen to my child! You would never forgive yourself! I swear to you: nothing will happen to you."

She read the fear in his eyes and lowered her head. "Yes," she said softly. "Yes, of course, I'll help you..."

Sir Cedric turned away, went to the drinks cabinet and poured Rona another whisky. She saw that he was furtively wiping his eyes. His hand trembled as he handed her the glass.

She took a hearty gulp. "Do I really have to go there alone?"

He nodded. "That's what the man on the phone said. He warned me. This was my last chance to get Susan back safely. Do you understand now that I don't want to risk anything more?"

"I understand that very well."

She felt the excitement leave her and her usual calm and confidence return.

"The best thing to do now is to explain to me exactly what you want me to do. There's no time to lose."

Kelford looked at her gratefully and quickly patted her hand. He explained to her the instructions the man had given him on the phone.

"You'll take my car and drive to Wimbledon Common. There you'll park in the square near the windmill. You're to remain seated in the car. The large suitcase containing the money will be on the back seat. They will bring Susan to the car, you hand over the suitcase and Susan stays with you. Then you'll come back here with her immediately."

"How will they recognise me?"

"They know my car. Besides, I doubt there are any other cars there at this time of night."

He pressed the bell button beside the fireplace and instructed the butler, who appeared a moment later, to put the suitcase into the car. Rona, still nervous despite herself, asked Kelford some questions about the operation of his car. Then they followed the butler, who had already disappeared down the stairs.

Before they went down, Sir Cedric Kelford put his hand on Rona's arm and held her back for a moment. "Whatever happens now," he said, deeply moved, "for what you are about to do, Rona, I shall be forever in your debt." In a sudden emotion he embraced her and kissed her tenderly on the cheek.

Three minutes later, Rona drove off. In the rear-view mirror she saw Sir Cedric Kelford standing motionless at the edge of the pavement in front of his house, staring after her.

The streets were empty. Her thoughts returned to the lonely man who had begged her for help.

Until that evening, she had only thought of him as a powerful businessman who had grown hard in the constant struggle for success. He seemed friendly to her, but sober and cool. Now she knew that behind that icy exterior with which he surrounded himself there were very tender feelings and a warm-heartedness that she had never suspected to find in him. She admitted to herself that never before had a man impressed her so deeply.

As she drove down Wimbledon Parkside, she realised that she was going well over the speed limit. She reduced her speed. It could only be minutes before she reached the square at the windmill.

***

Sergeant O'Donovan had followed Rona from Danilo's Restaurant to Sir Cedric Kelford's house in Eaton Square. He had had the taxi stop at the next corner, paid the driver and slowly returned to the vicinity of the house to take up his post. He leaned in the shade of an outside staircase and watched as Kelford's front door was opened and the butler stowed a large suitcase in the car. He saw Rona come out with Kelford, get into the Rolls Royce alone and drive off.

O'Donovan waited until Kelford had gone back into the house. Then he ran to an open sports car parked outside a house nearby, which he'd noticed when he arrived.

Why had Rona come in a taxi and now driven off in Kelford's car? An instinct told O'Donovan that something important was going on. He had to go after her. He didn't hesitate for a moment to jump into the sports car. The driver had forgotten to lock the steering wheel. O'Donovan pressed the starter button and the engine started immediately.

The sergeant stepped on the accelerator and sped off in the direction where Rona had disappeared with Kelford's Rolls. At Sloane Street he got Kelford's car in sight. Traffic was light and it was easy for O'Donovan not to lose sight of the Rolls Royce.

The girl is really pushing it, he thought. But I've got to keep up with her.

O'Donovan now felt remorse for having appropriated someone else's sports car without permission. But what else could I do in this situation, he asked himself? Houston will understand, but will the bosses in Scotland Yard let me get away with it when they find out that I have, as they will say, taken the law into my own hands? Oh, the devil take them all! It's success that counts. If something goes wrong, I'm just out of luck.

He chuckled at the thought that the sports car driver might have alerted the police by now and that he, O'Donovan, might be caught by a traffic patrol – a policeman as a car thief for official reasons.

He saw the Rolls Royce turning in the direction of the windmill. He stopped and waited for a few minutes. Then he too drove slowly into the large car park and stopped behind two other cars parked about sixty yards from the Rolls.

He switched off the lights, opened the door and pulled it shut again, pretending by the sound that he had left the car. He ducked down in the driver's seat. Only a few minutes later did he quietly open the door and slide out.

***

Rona saw a sports car roll into the car park. It looked somehow familiar, but she couldn't remember where and when she had seen it before. She heard a car door slam in the distance. After that it was quiet. Nothing moved in the square. The silence and the darkness oppressed her. What should she do if someone attacked her? Suppose the gangsters snatched the money case from her without handing over the child? What could she do about it? Nothing. Except to try to see the men, to memorise every detail of their appearance, as far as that was possible in this darkness.

She waited. Still there was no sound. She felt her heart pounding.

I must hold on, she suggested to herself. It's about little Susan, it's about Kelford. The thought of him gave her new confidence. She succeeded in conquering the rising fear. Suddenly she heard footsteps. They were approaching from the opposite side of the car park, where several unlit cars were parked.

Before she knew it, a man was standing next to her car window. He tapped softly on the window and she rolled it down. Her breath quickened.

She had to suppress a cry as the man leaned down towards her. He wore a hat, pulled low on his forehead. And a scarf tied over the lower half of his face. He was wearing a raincoat.

"Would you like to get out, please," he said politely. His voice was unrecognisable. Rona couldn't remember ever hearing that voice before.

Rona obeyed. Her knees trembled, but she forced herself to remain calm. If her nerves failed now, if she made a mistake, Kelford's and Susan's last chance was gone.

The man turned his head away from her and asked, "Where's the suitcase?"

"On the back seat," Rona replied obediently.

"Stay there," the masked man ordered and opened the rear door.

He pulled the suitcase out a little and let the locks snap open. Rona remained motionless in her position. The man quickly checked the contents of the suitcase, flipped the lid shut, pulled the heavy suitcase all the way out and put it down beside him.

He raised his hand. "This way," he said shortly.

Rona followed him to a narrow side path that led away from the car park. Hadn't Kelford explained that Susan would be taken to the car? But she thought it better not to ask any questions. She couldn't have said how long they walked. Maybe two, three minutes. It seemed like an eternity to her. A medium-sized limousine was parked between a small group of bushes. The masked man signalled Rona to stop, set the suitcase down, took a key from his pocket and opened the car door. He leaned into the car and pulled up the lock knob of the rear door. Then he straightened up and opened it from the outside.

"Come on, Susan," he whispered. "This lady here will take you home."

The little girl came crawling slowly out of the car. Susan yawned and stretched her arms. "I want to go to bed," she said in her bright voice.

Rona squatted down and cradled the little girl in her arms. "Your daddy is waiting for you," she whispered in a failing voice. "Come on, I'll take you to him..."

"Go now!" the masked man then ordered. "Don't waste any time and make sure you get away! You know the way back to your car."

Rona took Susan by the hand and ran off with her as if their lives depended on it. The little girl beside her stumbled but still Rona pulled her along.

"Come on, Susan, come on!"

Only when they reached the Rolls Royce did her fear give way.

***

Sergeant O'Donovan had found a large bush behind which he took cover. From there he could keep an eye on the Rolls Royce without being seen himself. As Rona disappeared into the darkness with the masked man, O'Donovan wondered if he should follow them. He decided against it and waited. He saw Rona come back with the child. He waited until the Rolls Royce had reached the exit of the car park, hurried to the sports car and started it. A little later he had almost caught up with the Rolls. He kept about a hundred yards behind it. After about a mile, he saw a limousine turn into the main road from a side path. O'Donovan drove past. The powerful headlights of the sports car illuminated the man at the wheel of the limousine for a moment. The detective saw the hat pulled low on his face, the scarf in front of his mouth. That must be the man, he thought. He drove on quickly and watched in the rear-view mirror that the limousine also stayed on the main road.

After some time, O'Donovan slowed down and let the limousine overtake. Was the masked man surveilling Rona for some reason?

O'Donovan switched off his headlights and decided to follow him. They drove down Putney High Street and turned to cross the bridge.

As the gangster's car went through, the traffic lights changed to red. O'Donovan had to stop and watch as the limousine crossed the bridge and disappeared into a street on the other side.

The light turned green and O'Donovan drove on. But he didn't know whether the limousine had turned right into Chelsea or continued straight ahead along Fulham Road. He had to make a quick decision. He curved to the right and pressed his foot firmly on the accelerator. If the masked man had continued in that direction, there was still a chance of catching him at top speed.

About two miles further on, O'Donovan spotted a sedan. It looked to be the same car, but the sergeant wasn't sure if his assumption was correct.

There was no sign of Sir Cedric Kelford's big Rolls Royce. Presumably Rona Houston had driven across the

Fulham Road. O'Donovan remembered that he should have followed Rona according to his instructions. But the hunting fever had taken hold of him. Maybe I'm wrong, he thought, but then I'm the one who will have to answer for it.

The car in front of him had to stop at the traffic lights in the King's Road. O'Donovan pulled up close, hoping to catch a glimpse of the driver to make sure.

The man behind the wheel used the pause to pull the scarf off his face and light a cigarette.

O'Donovan recognised him immediately. The man was a pickpocket known to the police: "Finger" Phillips.

The light of the traffic light changed. The limousine drove on. O'Donovan followed it at some distance. He wondered why "Finger" Phillips was now getting involved in such big-time crimes as child abduction. Interesting, O'Donovan thought. He seemed to rule out the possibility that Phillips himself was the head of the kidnap gang. "Finger" Phillips was at most a foot slogger, nothing more.

***

Despite everything that had happened, Susan seemed quite normal. She didn't seem frightened or shy, but rather happy. Obviously the child hadn't realised what had happened at all during these past few days.

Rona spoke to Susan from time to time during the drive, but she didn't ask her any questions. At Fulham Road she spotted a phone box, stopped, asked Susan if she wanted to speak to her father, and pulled the child into the phone box with her.

Sir Cedric was overjoyed. "I can't tell you, Rona, how I feel!" he said after the little girl had spoken to him and Rona had taken the receiver. "Please, come here at once!"

"Right away," Rona promised. "But would you do me a favour, Sir Cedric?"

"Whatever you want!"

"Then please call my father and tell him what has happened. You can probably still reach him at Scotland Yard. He mentioned that he had to work late today."

"Why, yes, of course, Rona."

What will Dad say to Sir Cedric? pondered Rona as she drove through Knightsbridge. She slowed her pace, for she noticed Susan's eyes closing and the child drifting off to sleep. At the same moment that she stopped in front of the house in Eaton Square, the front door was yanked open and Sir Cedric Kelford came storming down the steps of the outside staircase.

Rona opened the door, switched on the overhead light and put her finger to her lips. "She's asleep, Sir Cedric..."

"Carry her to bed," she continued in a whisper. "But don't wake her. I'm sure that's for the best. When she wakes in her own bed in the morning, she won't even know what's happened. If she still remembers, she'll think she was dreaming."

Kelford nodded and took the sleeping child into his arms. She followed him into the house, went with him to the nursery and helped him tuck Susan into bed. They tiptoed out of the room.

On the way to the living room, Kelford squeezed her arm several times. "I don't know how to thank you, Rona," he said haltingly when he had closed the room door behind him. He swallowed. "Come on, Rona!" He led her to the rocking chair by the fire, pushed her into it and gently stroked her hair. She let it happen. She had to fight down her emotion.

Suddenly she looked up. "And now for a drink, Sir Cedric," she said, smiling through her tears. "I could certainly do with one."

And for the first time in a long time Sir Cedric Kelford smiled. "Forgive me, but I should have thought of that!" He looked her in the eye, and there was something in his gaze that made Rona blush. She lowered her head. He lightly brushed her arm as he walked past her to the drinks cabinet. Then they heard a car pull up.

A minute later Mike Houston was standing in the room. He walked towards his daughter. "Is everything all right, Rona?" he asked anxiously.

She nodded and he hugged her. Kelford squeezed Houston's hand. "If Rona hadn't helped me, I don't know what would have happened, Inspector!" He looked at Houston and then turned to Rona. "I hope you don't mind if we have some champagne now? If this isn't cause for celebration..."

While Kelford rang for the butler, Houston asked, "Did you notice if anyone followed you, Rona?"

Rona frowned, trying to remember. "I don't know, Dad," she finally said. "Why, should I?"

"Sergeant O'Donovan has been assigned to protect you. For days now he's been tailing you. We had to expect something would happen to you."

"Wait a minute," Rona said quickly. "I noticed a cream-coloured sports car out there by the windmill. And I think I saw it in the mirror on the way back. But I could be wrong. It could have been a coincidence. There are a lot of cars like that about."

Houston shrugged. "Maybe," he growled. "But I hope it was O'Donovan. Maybe he's got something out of it. But now tell me everything."

The butler appeared with the champagne and they toasted Sir Cedric on the rescue of his daughter.

"But now I must be off, back to the Yard," Houston said after a glance at his watch. "Will you come with me, Rona? I'll drive straight home afterwards then."

Kelford shook his head with a smile. "Dear Inspector, I hope you will allow me to take Rona home."

made a gesture of understanding with his hand.

d the glasses once more. "From now on, Rona is ...y family," Kelford said haltingly, handing her the glass.

Mike Houston finished his drink and rose. "I'll report to Superintendent Elder that your daughter's home safe and sound," he said in a matter-of-fact tone.

Kelford accompanied him out.

***

Scotland Yard had no news of O'Donovan. Houston called Superintendent Elder at home and gave him an account of the evening's events. He had hardly hung up the receiver when the telephone rang again and the watch commander in the hall reported to him the arrival of Bob Harridge.

"Send him up!"

Houston greeted Harridge in amazement. "Hello, Bob, what on earth are you doing here in the middle of the night?"

Bob Harridge was quite nervous. "I tried to reach you at home by phone just after Rona said goodbye. I'm sure you know we had dinner together tonight, at Danilo's," he added, explaining. "But unfortunately no one answered. So I called here and was told that you were coming back. I apologise for barging in like this."

Houston looked at him with interest. "Is it something important?"

Bob Harridge raised his hands and dropped them again. "I don't know if it's important. But it could be. You know, I was worried about Rona. I didn't know exactly where I stood with her. She seemed so different from usual. As soon as we finished dinner, she left. And I thought I'd give you a call and see how she was. Yes, and here I am..."

Houston smiled at Bob's eagerness. "It's all right, Bob. I just saw her twenty minutes ago."

Harridge looked relieved. "Thank goodness. That's a load off my mind, Inspector. She didn't seem very happy tonight. I even wondered if she," he faltered, "...if she'd learned anything about Dennis..."

"What do you mean?" asked Houston sharply.

Harridge screwed up his face and cradled his head. "I don't know, sir, it was just an impression. I may be mistaken. You know I'm very fond of Rona. I'd be sorry if she was involved in anything untoward or if anything should distress her."

"I'm sure she would appreciate your concern," Houston replied dryly.

"I know we haven't seen much of each other since she went on the stage and that Carl Knight guy came on the scene," Harridge continued, frowning. "But that wasn't because of me, and I've already told you I really like her..."

"I know, Bob."

Houston was interrupted by the ringing of the telephone.

"This is Sergeant O'Donovan, sir. I'm speaking from a phone box in Whitechapel Road. How is Miss Houston? Has she returned safely?"

"All's well," Houston assured him. "And what about you?"

Quickly O'Donovan described to him how he had followed the limousine. "You remember 'Finger' Phillips, don't you, Inspector? I tailed him to a small tobacco shop in Malabar Street here in Whitechapel. He parked his car in front of the side entrance, turned off the lights and locked the car. It looks like he is staying in the house overnight. Maybe he lives there. He must have taken the suitcase with the money inside with him. It's not in the car any more."

Houston reached for a notepad. "Repeat the address!"

He wrote it down. "Get back there as soon as you can!" His voice suddenly had an undertone of excitement.

He put the phone down. "I'm sorry, Bob, but I've got work to do. Don't worry about Rona. I'll look after her all right."

He waited until Harridge had left the room, picked up the house phone and alerted Scotland Yard's Flying Squad.

Ten minutes later, police cars roared through the deserted streets of Whitechapel. The driver of the car Houston was in knew Malabar Street. Houston directed him to park in a levelled rubble lot near the house O'Donovan had indicated. Other vehicles cordoned off the street. The driver remained in the car and two men accompanied Houston. They found O'Donovan in a gateway almost directly opposite the tobacco shop.

"There's a light in the back of the shop," he whispered to Houston. "And further up the stairs, too."

Houston waited a few minutes until the policemen who were to guard the back of the house must have reached their posts. Then he crossed the street with O'Donovan.

As they passed, O'Donovan pointed to the limousine parked in front of the side entrance. The side door apparently led to the flats.

Houston looked in vain for a bell and knocked hard on the door. Nothing moved. He knocked again, and a second later they heard heavy footsteps. The door opened and a man in shirt sleeves stood before them. He appeared to be about fifty years old.

"What is it? What d'yer want?" he asked roughly. His voice was low. "Don't you know the shop is closed at this time of night?"

Houston looked at him for a moment. Then he said, "George Waters, look at you! You remember me, Waters, don't you? You remember... that bank robbery gone wrong back in Holborn..."

The other took a step back.

"You can't pin nothing on me," he stammered. "I'm clean, Inspector, absolutely clean, for years now! I've got my little shop here, and otherwise..."

"All right, all right," Houston interrupted him. "We've nothing against you at all. But we'd like to have a word with 'Finger' Phillips. If you don't happen to be in on the story..."

Waters looked at him anxiously. "I don't know what it's about, Inspector. I'm just renting him a room. There's no law against that, is there? I don't know anything about him, not a thing."

"All the better for you, Waters. Where is he?"

Waters led them to the foot of the stairs and pointed to a door on the first floor. Houston nodded to O'Donovan to accompany him.

"And no funny business, Waters," he said quietly over his shoulder. "We have the house surrounded."

Quietly he and O'Donovan walked up the stairs. Houston knocked on the door of the room. From inside they heard the sound of a cupboard door being slammed.

"Open up, Phillips!" shouted Houston loudly.

"It's not locked," said the man in the room.

Houston turned the door knob and entered, closely followed by O'Donovan. No sooner had they entered the room than a man jumped out from behind the door and tried to escape. With a diving leap, O'Donovan threw himself on him. After a short struggle, "Finger" Phillips was overwhelmed.

"A bit out of condition, eh, Finger?" grinned O'Donovan and threw him into an armchair. "And if you move now, my friend, you're in for a treat!"

Houston looked around the shabbily furnished room. There was only one place Phillips could have put the suitcase, if he'd taken it to the room, in the cupboard.

"Where's the key?" asked Houston.

Reluctantly, Phillips fumbled in his waistcoat pocket and tossed Houston a key. The suitcase lay under a pile of old clothes and dirty laundry on the cupboard floor. Houston opened it, took a quick look inside and closed it again.

"Is there anything you'd like to say about it?" he asked, turning to Phillips.

"I didn't know what's in it," Phillips replied sullenly in a dragging voice. "I just picked it up for someone."

"The pure lamb," said Sergeant O'Donovan, "but you're lying, man! I saw you hand over the Kelford kid myself."

"We know more than you think, Phillips," Houston said calmly. "I suggest you come clean. Or you could be in for a hell of a lot worse for a pretty long time."

Phillips's face twitched. "I was just doing what I was told, that's all," he assured them, gesticulating fiercely.

Houston didn't let up. "Where are you supposed to take the case? Think carefully about your answer. Don't try to trick us!"

Phillips shook his head. "Nowhere. Really, nowhere. He's going to pick it up."

"When?"

"Maybe in a day or two, maybe later. What do I know?"

"And who is he?" asked Houston.

Before Phillips could answer, they heard quick footsteps from outside, approaching the back of the house. A door was pushed open downstairs. Houston ran out of the room and bent over the banister. The man, who had already set foot on the first step, looked up at him. He was surprised and confused. Their eyes met. Silently they looked at each other for a few seconds.

Calmly Houston said: "Well, what are you doing in this area? Are you looking for something?"

Chapter Ten

Carl Knight stared motionlessly up the stairs. Mike Houston looked down at him calmly. "What are you doing here?" he repeated.

The writer made no reply. Slowly Houston walked down the stairs towards him. Knight withdrew the foot he had placed on the first step.

"I didn't know you knew your way around this part of the world, Mr Knight," Houston continued. "What are you doing here?"

He was standing close to him now. Suddenly an ironic smile slid across Knight's face. "I would have expected you to figure it out on your own, Inspector. After all, I'm a writer. I study local colour here. I need an interesting setting for my next play, and this neighbourhood, you'll admit, is very good for providing the background for dramatic entanglements."

Houston looked at him doubtfully. Although Knight had produced a grin intended to demonstrate cheerfulness and impartiality, the author had gone pale.

"But why are you coming to this house of all places?" drilled Houston further.

Knight narrowed his gaze for a moment. "Perhaps I shouldn't say anything about that, Inspector. I don't want to cause Waters any inconvenience. After all, his shop has been officially closed for five hours now."

"What are you getting at?" asked Houston impatiently.

"Well," Knight pressed on, "George Waters sells me a few packs of cigarettes now and then, there at the side door, when his shop has long been closed. I know that's against the law. But I hope you won't hold it against him. He keeps to the closing time. He makes an exception for me once in a while. A chain smoker like me is a particularly good customer for him, that's obvious. Go on, turn a blind eye for once, Inspector!"

On the contrary, Houston thought, now I'll keep my eyes open even more! "Have you seen Waters yet, Knight?"

"No, he doesn't seem to be around."

"Stop right there," Houston ordered. He walked back up the stairs to halfway up. "Bring the man down, O'Donovan," he called.

At the top the door was opened. Sergeant O'Donovan pushed "Finger" Phillips in front of him. As a precaution, the detective handcuffed him, and Houston observed that Knight noticed immediately.

When O'Donovan and Phillips reached the bottom of the stairs, "Finger" seemed to recognise the writer. Knight looked at him calmly. Neither of them said a word.

Knight glared after the prisoner while O'Donovan led him out. Another officer came in, ran up to the room and returned with the suitcase of money that Phillips had tried to hide in the cupboard.

Houston had been silent the whole time. "Well, is that dramatic enough for you, Mr Knight?" he asked at last. "Or would you like to be offered something more?"

Knight didn't respond to his tone. "Is there a police raid going on or something like that?" he inquired.

"Do you know the man who was just led past you?" Houston wanted to know without answering his question.

The author shook his head. "I've never seen him before in my life. Why was he handcuffed?"

The Inspector looked at him sharply. "He's involved in the kidnapping of Sir Cedric Kelford's daughter."

"Oh God!"

Knight seemed very much taken aback. "Yes, that affair. I'd almost forgotten about her..."

"Scotland Yard, on the other hand, has a pretty good memory," Houston replied. "I hope you were telling the truth when you claimed you didn't know the man."

Protesting, Knight raised his hand. "How dare you, Inspector..."

He interrupted himself. The door from the hallway to the shop had opened, and the bearded George Waters, still shirt-sleeved, stood on the threshold.

"I have nothing to do with all this, Inspector," he groaned hoarsely. "Really I haven't. 'Finger' Phillips asked me to rent him a room. That's all I know." His face was grey with anxiety.

"And you wouldn't happen to know this gentleman here, I suppose?" asked Houston, pointing at Knight.

Waters' eyes narrowed. Knight opened his mouth to say something, but the shopkeeper beat him to it. "I've never seen him before in my life, Inspector. Is he a mate of Phillips?"

"That remains to be seen," Houston grumbled.

Carl Knight gestured at Waters. "But of course you know me! You've been selling me cigarettes for many weeks now, haven't you?"

Stubbornly, Waters shook his head. "I don't remember doing that," he insisted.

Houston grabbed him by the arm. "The best thing is to come with me to the police station. We'll find out how much you remember," he said energetically. Then he turned to Knight. "And I'll expect you at Scotland Yard tomorrow morning. Hopefully by then we'll see a little more clearly."

He pushed the protesting Waters out of the door and left Knight standing.

***

When Houston entered the police station the next morning, the sergeant on duty received him with a worried expression.

"What's up? Anything unpleasant happened?" asked Houston immediately.

The sergeant nodded. "You won't get anything out of that Phillips character, Inspector. He's dead."

"How the hell...?" began Houston grimly.

"He had a poison capsule on him, and it..."

"But he'd been searched!"

Perplexed, the sergeant raised his hands. "He must have had it hidden in his mouth."

Houston uttered an expletive and paced the office impatiently. "Of all the times, when we thought we were so close to a solution, this has to happen!" he hissed. Then he sank into silence.

For a long time the sergeant didn't dare address the furious Inspector. "I'm sorry, sir," he finally said quietly. "Do you think it will be useful for you to talk to Waters?"

Houston nodded, and the sergeant disappeared to bring Waters up from the cells. Until he returned with the arrested man, Houston drummed the fingers of his right hand on the tabletop.

"Sit down, Waters, and tell the truth – that's what I advise you to do!"

The interrogation went on for over half an hour without Houston being able to extract any useful information from the dealer.

Waters maintained that he'd never seen Carl Knight until the previous night.

Disappointed, the Inspector returned to Scotland Yard. Superintendent Elder had already been briefed on the latest events.

"Thank God that at least the child is back home safe and sound," he said with relief. But as he continued, his face darkened. "It doesn't look like we're going to clear up all the murders committed in connection with the Kelford affair any time soon though, I'm afraid, Houston. Or do you feel we are close to solving them?"

Houston breathed heavily.

"Have you learned anything from this chap Phillips?" asked Elder.

The Inspector told him about Phillips' death.

Elder growled. "So he committed suicide, did he? That suggests he must have been something more than a stooge. Why else would he have had reason to take his own life?"

"Don't forget another point, sir," Houston objected. "Phillips may have been very disturbed. I think he was afraid, mortally afraid. Of the head of this gang. We caught him with the case full of money. From the point of view of his employer, Phillips had failed. And now he feared the revenge of the gang leader, who had given away his bargaining chip, the child, and now wouldn't get the money either. In other words, the main culprit behind the whole thing has taken all the risks for nothing, for nothing at all. His crimes haven't paid off. So Phillips had every reason to be afraid of this man, who we know stops at nothing. I think that's why he killed himself."

Elder agreed with him. "It might have been that way. Though I don't see how anything could have happened to Phillips while he was in custody. But it's idle to worry about that now. At least we have some consolation." He returned to the starting point of the conversation. "The child is back."

Houston stood up. "Yes," he said. "But what about the murders! Nobbler Williams. My son Dennis. Mary Latimer. Mrs Spedro..."

"You're right, Houston, there's a lot of work still to be done. The Assistant Commissioner has scheduled a conference for tonight. He wants to discuss with us the latest developments in this affair."

137

"I'll be there on time," Houston replied and left the room dejectedly.

***

The evening conference went differently than Houston had expected. All day he hadn't been able to shake off the fear that the Assistant Chief of Scotland Yard would give him and his staff hell.

However, the Assistant Commissioner received them kindly. He congratulated Houston on the fact that he and his men had extracted the ten thousand pounds ransom from the kidnapper.

"And now, Houston, I'd like to know who you think is behind all this. You have formed a theory, haven't you?"

Houston nodded. "I have, but I think that it is perhaps a little too early to talk about it now, sir. I'm not at all sure in my own mind. Theories are all very well. But as for proof – that's what's lacking.... Please, can you give me a little more time? I may soon be able to report an arrest to you."

Superintendent Elder intervened. "Don't you think, Houston, that it is time to do something about this Knight chap? We," he pointed to the Assistant Commissioner and himself, "suspect him of murdering your son and Mrs Spedro."

"It's not so easy to prove anything against him, sir," Houston pointed out. "In fact, I doubt very much that he is the murderer of Mrs Spedro. I discovered that she was a kleptomaniac. She had a lot of stolen things on her when we found her. She stole my daughter's scarf when she visited Knight's flat. She was wearing that scarf when she visited the flat of the mysterious Mr Arnold, who has yet to turn up, and that's where someone strangled her using that scarf."

"Is that just theory at the moment – or…?" asked the Assistant Commissioner.

"Not very much more than that as yet," Houston admitted.

Elder steered the conversation back to the writer. "Knight could have followed Mrs Spedro and killed her in the flat at Ainsworth Court," he insisted.

"It's not out of the question," Houston conceded.

"It looks to me as if Knight is this mysterious Mr Arnold," Elder growled. "I don't trust that fellow from here to there." He pointed to the wall.

The Assistant Commissioner closed the files in front of him shut. "All right, Houston, go ahead. But I want you to keep in touch with me. If necessary, you can call me at home."

***

As Big Ben, the clock tower of the Houses of Parliament, struck ten Houston left Scotland Yard. He decided to take a short walk to get some fresh air.

He saw a man standing under a lantern on the bank of the Thames. He was looking across the river, arms folded, one hand on his chin. He didn't wear a hat so the wind had ruffled his hair.

As Houston came closer, he recognised Dr Spedro. The doctor woke from his stupor and looked at Houston. He didn't seem in the least surprised to have the Inspector in front of him.

"Hello," he said in a strained voice. "What are you doing here, Doctor?"

Spedro shrugged his shoulders. "I don't think I know exactly myself. I couldn't come to any conclusion, you see. I thought about going to the Yard to see you. But then – what's the point of it all? My wife's dead and I..."

He broke off. All the self-confidence Houston had known in him previously had fallen away. Dr Spedro looked distressed and confused.

"And what would you have told me if you had come to see me at the Yard?" inquired Houston.

"It's about the yellow windmill," Dr Spedro said quietly.

Houston couldn't see Spedro's face clearly in the dim glow of the lantern. But there was something in the doctor's tone that made him sit up and take notice.

"Shall we talk here?" asked Houston. "Or wouldn't we be better off going over to Scotland Yard and taking a statement there?"

Dr Spedro hesitated for a moment before replying, "If you don't mind, we'll go to your office, Inspector."

"But of course."

Silently they walked side by side, each preoccupied with his own thoughts.

In his office, Houston offered the doctor a cigarette and telephoned for a sergeant to take Spedro's statement.

The officer took a seat in the corner of the room behind Spedro. He nodded to Houston that he was ready. "So, doctor, what do you want to tell me?"

Spedro inhaled the cigarette smoke deeply and exhaled it again.

"Over ten years ago, when I came to this country, I was in a very bad way," he began. "My studies were expensive, I had to live too, and I only earned a few pounds doing unskilled work in a hospital. I didn't really have any choice but to go into debt if I wanted to keep up with my studies. I desperately needed two hundred pounds. A bank wouldn't give me a penny. So I went to a money lender. He even suggested how I could earn money."

He hesitated. "What he asked me to do was against the law, but..." He fumed hastily.

"You accepted his proposal?" asked Houston.

"Yes, I did. I was given the address of a country house in Hertfordshire. I went there and met a young man who asked me to get him a certain narcotic. I had the opportunity to do this at the hospital where I worked. I stole the dope and so..."

140

"I see," Houston urged. "So what?"

"Years went by. I had long since finished my studies, settled in Wimpole Street and become a respected doctor. My practice flourished. Then one day the young man from those days turned up at my house. He came to remind me of our first meeting..."

"You mean he blackmailed you," Houston interrupted him.

Spedro nodded. "First he demanded money. Then, realising that even my wealth is not unlimited, he helped himself in other ways."

Houston leaned forward. "Doctor – do we know this young man?"

Spedro looked him in the eye. "His name is Carl Knight."

Houston jumped to his feet. He clasped his hands around the back of his desk chair. "Why didn't you come to us sooner with all this, Doctor?"

Dr Spedro ran his hand over his forehead. "You must understand – I was doing very well. As long as Knight didn't make excessive demands, it seemed more sensible for me to obey him."

"And then he started to exploit you for other purposes," Houston picked up the thread again.

"Yes, he borrowed my car quite often. That worried me because I had no idea what he needed it for. He had my car the night Nobbler Williams was run over..."

"I had the impression right away that Knight was the one who did it," Houston muttered.

"After a while," Spedro continued, "my wife noticed that there was something wrong with me. Eventually she realised that I was being blackmailed by Knight. She was a very courageous woman, and she went straight to confront him. He told her he was just a tool of another man called Arnold who lived in Ainsworth Court. She needed to talk to this Arnold.

141

So my wife went along with it. But when she went to Ainsworth Court later, Carl Knight was waiting for her there."

"Wait a minute, Doctor," Houston interposed. "Do you mean Knight is the mysterious Mr Arnold?"

Spedro laughed bitterly. "I don't mean that, Inspector. I know it! One night when he came to see me again, he'd drunk a lot. And at my place he downed a few more glasses of whisky. Then he bragged about how he'd tricked you. It was about a typewriter that he sold and bought back, changing his appearance a little and posing as Mr Arnold."

"So this Arnold character was a fabrication all the time," Houston mused. "Carl Knight's a cunning little so-and-so coming up with something like that, it has to be said. And what was his relationship with your patient Mary Latimer?"

"He had a thing for her, as they say. She was crazy about him. But eventually he got tired of Mary, and at the same time he was very worried because she knew a lot about him.... She realised that he was very interested in your daughter, Inspector, and that made her even more dangerous to him. He feared that in her jealousy she was capable of anything. He saw only one way out: he forced me to put Mary in my nursing home, on some pretext or other...

"Yes," Spedro recalled. "But she got away. The effect of the anaesthetic I had given her wore off sooner than expected and Mary managed to escape. She went to the television studio to warn your daughter Rona about Knight. But unfortunately, Knight beat her to it. He murdered Mary and hid her body in your daughter's car."

Houston looked at the doctor scrutinisingly. Dr Spedro's face looked sunken. But his fingers, which had been nervously playing with the cigarette at the beginning of his story, were now resting calmly on the tabletop. Obviously it meant a great relief for Spedro to finally get everything off his chest.

"What do you know about the yellow windmill Mary was clutching when we found her?" Houston continued the conversation.

"It was stolen from my consulting room," Dr Spedro explained. "I missed it after Knight had come to me to force me to admit Mary to the nursing home."

Houston frowned. "But when I came to you, the windmill was still on the shelf!"

Dr Spedro shook his head. "What you saw was another specimen exactly like the first. I had taken the second windmill from my wife's room. I feared that Carl Knight wanted to arouse the police's suspicion of me and had stolen the yellow windmill for that purpose. Therefore, I immediately took my precautions."

"You do realise, don't you, that you have considerably hindered and complicated the investigations of the police, don't you, Doctor?" Mike Houston said emphatically. "But I don't want to get into all that now. After all, you came here voluntarily this evening to tell us everything you know. And that's a great help to us."

Spedro indicated a bow as he sat. "I thank you, Inspector, but in some corner of your heart you will perhaps understand me a little. I was under pressure, I was at a loss for a long time. Knight had me in the palm of his hand, he could destroy my very existence. What was I supposed to do? But now, since the death of my wife, I don't care about anything..."

"Okay," Houston said. "And now about the kidnapping of little Susan Kelford. What do you know about that? Do you think Knight was responsible for that too?"

Dr Spedro lit a new cigarette. "I don't know anything more specific, but I'm pretty sure he was the culprit. He had my car that day..."

Houston sat back. "It's remarkable, actually, that such a busy young man still found the time to write a play and rewrite it during television production," he stated dryly.

"You are mistaken there, Inspector," Dr Spedro enlightened him. "The play is not his at all."

"What?"

"No. Mary Latimer wrote it, not Carl Knight."

Houston let out a whistle. "Why, that's..."

"You can see how much she was under his influence," Spedro said. "He managed to convince her that this play would have a much better chance of being performed if it was presented under his name. In doing so, he provided himself with a new façade – the busy playwright. He put on a big show when he was asked to rewrite one scene or another. To do that, he said, he needed peace and solitude, he could only do that at home. In reality, Mary Latimer was the one who did the work. He himself had no ability to do it at all. I learned all this from Mary Latimer herself."

Dr Spedro tugged at his cuffs. "You can take it from me, Inspector, this Carl Knight is the man you are looking for. And I must confess to you, I won't be sorry if he goes behind bars."

He pulled out his handkerchief and dabbed his forehead.

Houston asked him a series of more questions. But he couldn't find a gap, or a weak spot in Dr Spedro's account. The doctor knew an answer to every additional question that matched what had been said before.

"I must ask you to remain at our disposal, Doctor."

As Spedro left, Houston was left feeling that the investigation had now entered its decisive stage. He reached for the phone and requested an arrest warrant for Carl Knight. Then he alerted Sergeant O'Donovan, "Wait for me in the car outside the Yard."

***

144

On the way to Carl Knight's flat in the Cromwell Road, Houston briefed the sergeant in broad terms about the doctor's statement. They stopped outside the police station in charge and took with them two officers who knew the area intimately. When they reached their destination, Houston posted them at the back of the house.

The house was in darkness and the main entrance was locked. Houston rang the doorbell twice. After a while he heard shuffling footsteps. The porter's wife opened the door. She had slipped an old coat over her nightgown.

Houston showed his ID. "Is Mr Knight home?"

"I don't know," she said sullenly, leading him to Knight's flat door.

"There it is. Go see for yourself!"

She disappeared.

Houston knocked on the door, and a few moments later it was opened.

Carl Knight was fully dressed despite the late hour. The Inspector immediately noticed that there was a mackintosh over a chair in the hallway.

"This is a bit of a late visit, Inspector," Knight began. "I was just packing."

He led Houston and O'Donovan into the living room.

"Are you going somewhere?" asked Houston.

It didn't escape his notice that Knight looked even paler than the last time they'd met. "Yes, just for a few days."

"Well," Houston said, "you'll have to allow us to ask you a few more questions before you leave..."

Knight leaned against a shelf and folded his arms. "You seem so solemn, Inspector. Don't you want to tell me first why you're here at such a late hour..."

Houston stood between Knight and the door. "I had a lengthy conversation with Dr Spedro today, Knight. A very interesting conversation, as a matter of fact." He straightened to his full height. "I thought you should know the result of that conversation at once."

He was silent for a moment. Knight stared at him. But he didn't give up his seemingly calm attitude.

Houston continued to speak. "I charge you with the murder of Mary Latimer and Margaretta Spedro. There are some other charges that will be made against you, but I don't want to go into those at the moment. I draw your attention to the fact that anything you say from now on can be used against you. Of course, you may seek the assistance of a lawyer."

After this prescribed routine warning, he said calmly, "You'd better get your hat and coat now, Mr Knight..."

Carl Knight moved away from the shelf and walked across the large room.

"That Spedro must be crazy. I've had that suspicion for a long time. The guy's not all there in the head, Inspector! Tell me, haven't you noticed that yet?"

"On the contrary," Houston replied gruffly, "I'm convinced that he spoke the truth. And for that conviction I have my reasons. Now come on, Knight!"

Carl Knight made a throwing-away motion with his hand, as if to indicate that everyone but him was apparently not quite in their right minds.

"Alright." His voice sounded sullen. "If you insist... But I suppose you'll allow me to go to my bedroom. I need a few more things to take with me. Just give me five minutes."

"Two minutes," Houston ordered. "That'll do. And leave the bedroom door open!"

Knight nodded and went into the bedroom, which faced the street.

Houston watched him through the open door. He saw Knight pick up a spectacles case and then step to a small

146

table. Suddenly he heard a glass clink. Knight brought his hand to his mouth.

Houston rushed into the bedroom. O'Donovan came after him. Before they reached Knight, he collapsed.

"He must have swallowed a poison capsule!" screamed Houston. "Run down quickly, O'Donovan, and get the others in case we have to carry Knight to the car. It might still do some good to have a doctor pump his stomach!"

O'Donovan had already hurried out. Houston ran into the hallway and phoned for an ambulance. He hung up the phone and heard O'Donovan and the others coming up the stairs. Houston ran back to the bedroom. He opened his eyes. The window curtains were billowing in the wind. The room was deserted. Carl Knight was gone.

Chapter Eleven

"Damn it!" growled Inspector Houston. "This is where he was lying on the floor. It looked like he'd been poisoned. If only we hadn't fallen for his trick!"

But he couldn't have got far, he reassured himself. He quickly looked around the room. The window curtains were billowing in the breeze. The windows must have been open. Houston remembered clearly that they had been closed before. He ran over and pulled the curtains apart. They covered a balcony door. Houston pulled them all the way open and stepped out. The first thing he saw was the beam of a powerful flashlight. The beam came from below, from a spot in front of the house. Houston bent over the iron railings and his gaze followed the beam of light. It was directed at a dark figure that seemed to be stuck to the wall about fifteen yards away from him, ten yards above the ground.

Good thing we have the house surrounded, Houston thought, the men below are on their guard. Carl Knight had climbed up onto a stone ledge that stretched all around the building for decoration. It was amazing that he had come this far in the few minutes of his breakneck escape. The ornamental cornice was only about ten inches wide. Knight seemed determined to take every risk in the book. If he fell, he could break his neck. He was probably going to try to escape through one of the neighbouring flats. Houston saw the shadowy figure sway for a few seconds; he heard a half-sounding exclamation. Then Knight had regained his composure. He probably clawed his hands into the rough plaster to find his footing above the deadly depths. Houston wondered if he should call out to him to give himself up. But Knight would be frightened and fall. And he, Houston, wanted to catch this criminal alive, to be able to interrogate him, to clear up the mystery of the yellow windmill once and for all.

He waited and saw Sergeant O'Donovan step out of the front door. "Watch him, O'Donovan!" he called to him.

He ran out of the flat and rang the doorbell of the neighbouring flat. It took a few minutes before a sleepy young man appeared. He stared at the Inspector.

"Police? Why...?"

Houston quickly explained to him what it was about. "Out on the wall, outside my flat? My goodness, Inspector! Come in!"

They walked down the corridor, the young man pushing open a door to a room. "There's the window."

"Don't turn on the light!" ordered Houston.

Quietly he opened the window. He stuck his head out and looked to the left, in the direction where Carl Knight must be standing, close to the window, on the ledge. The spot was empty. Houston looked down. The beam of the torch that had followed Carl Knight earlier was now aimed at a bush in the front garden. O'Donovan and another man hurried towards the bushes.

"What's going on?" shouted Houston.

"The masonry gave way under him, sir."

"Is he unconscious?"

"Probably. In a fall from that height!"

"I'll be right down." Two minutes later Mike Houston was bending over Carl Knight. He looked into the distorted face. Blood poured from several deep head wounds and ran over his closed eyes.

Carl Knight wouldn't be able to answer any questions, at least for several hours, if ever. He was still unconscious when the ambulance arrived. The police doctor took one look at the motionless, contorted figure, looked at Houston and shook his head.

The Inspector gave him his phone number and asked him to call if Carl Knight woke from his unconsciousness. He returned to Knight's flat with Sergeant O'Donovan. "We need to search every nook and cranny, O'Donovan."

Silently they set to work, rummaging through cupboards and drawers with practised grips, emptying out vases, lifting each object to see if anything was hidden underneath.

Houston sorted out some papers whose contents seemed to be related to Knight's criminal activity and put them in his briefcase. He wanted to examine them later at his leisure.

After two hours they ended the search. They left a constable in the flat and O'Donovan drove Houston home in a police car.

"Looks like we should be able to close the case soon," O'Donovan said as they pulled up in front of Houston's house.

Mike Houston shook his head doubtfully. "I'm not so sure, Sergeant. There are still a lot of unanswered questions. And whether Knight can answer them all, even if he were physically able – I don't know..."

Yawning, he got out. "Well, good night, Sergeant." He took the briefcase with the papers he had secured from Knight's flat and went into the house. When he opened the door to the living room, he stopped in surprise. Rona wasn't alone. Bob Harridge was sitting next to her, talking at her. They lifted their heads. Rona immediately saw from her father that something extraordinary must have taken place.

"What's the matter?" she asked tensely.

Houston nodded. He put the briefcase down, dropped into an armchair and told in short bursts what had happened. Harridge seemed very interested in his narrative.

"Well, at last," he said after Houston had concluded his account, "I suppose that clears up the mystery of the yellow windmill, Inspector?"

"I'm afraid not..." said Houston. "But I expect something else will happen soon that will bring us closer to solving the case."

Bob frowned. "I don't understand, Inspector."

Rona, too, looked at Houston in amazement.

Before he could answer, the phone rang. He went out into the hallway and picked it up.

"Knight has regained consciousness," the doctor reported. "But his injuries are very severe and..."

"Will he pull through?" asked Houston quickly.

"I don't think so, Inspector. But listen – he did a few minutes ago..."

The doctor continued to speak. Houston listened with increasing interest.

Suddenly he heard the living room door behind him, turned, and saw Bob Harridge coming into the hallway, followed by Rona.

"Just a minute, Doctor!" Houston put his hand over the shell of the telephone.

"I just wanted to say goodbye, Inspector," Bob Harridge said. "Good night." He left the flat.

Houston returned to his phone call. "Yes, Doctor – what happened next?"

Rona had stopped beside him. He looked at her as he listened to the doctor's last words. Then he hung up.

"Carl Knight wants to see you, Rona."

Her eyes widened. "Me? Why would he want to see me?"

"The doctor thinks maybe he wants to confide in you. The doctor doesn't know any specifics. He doesn't think Knight will live to see the day out, by the way."

"My God!" Rona breathed heavily. "I never thought Carl..."

She fell silent. "Of course I'll go," she then said.

Houston put a hand on her arm. "I'll come with you, Rona. Put on a warm coat. It's getting cold out."

Lowering her head, she went into her room. Houston returned to the living room.

When Rona reappeared in the hallway a few minutes later, the doorbell rang and she opened it.

Bob Harridge stood before her. "I'm sorry to bother you again." He spoke breathlessly. "But I'm afraid I took the wrong briefcase."

"Come in, Bob!"

They went into the living room. Mike Houston sat leaning back in his armchair, drinking a glass of whisky. He stood up and put the glass down. "Back again, Bob?"

"Excuse me, sir. But there's been a slight mix-up..."

He lifted the briefcase in his hand. "These things do look alike!"

He looked around. "Ah, there's mine!" He took the bag, which was leaning against an armchair.

Houston and Rona accompanied him out.

"And excuse me again, please, sir," Bob Harridge took his leave. "I should have realised sooner, of course, that I'd picked up the wrong briefcase. But I just wasn't paying attention."

"Never mind, lad," Houston assured him. "Mistakes like that happen."

A few minutes after Harridge left them, Houston and Rona set off for the hospital. Houston steered Rona's small car quickly through the night's quiet streets. After barely half an hour, they arrived at the hospital.

A nurse led Rona to Knight's room. Houston stayed behind in a waiting room. Deep in thought he lit a cigarette.

Rona seemed very agitated when she returned. Houston silently took her by the arm and led her back to the car. He helped her in, closed the door, walked around to the other side and got in. Only then did he ask, "Why did he push so hard for you to come to see him?"

Rona reached for his hand, feeling his daughter trembling, and stroked her fingers.

"It was because..." She interrupted herself and swallowed. "He swore to me he had nothing to do with Dennis's death, Dad. And I believe him. Why should he have lied, now. He knows he's going to die soon. The murders of Nobbler Williams, Mary Latimer, Mrs Spedro, the kidnapping of Susan Kelford – he admitted to all of that. But over and over again he begged me to believe him, that it wasn't him who killed Dennis!"

Houston's face hardened. He thought of his dead son Dennis. In the armchair. Shot to death. And in the wooden frame close above the screen of the television box: the drawing of a yellow windmill.

Rona was silent. Only her breathing could be heard.

"Why did he kill Nobbler Williams?" asked Houston after a pause.

"Carl had learned that you once did Williams a favour. I don't know what it was."

"That's right," Houston interrupted her. "I turned a blind eye once, as far as Nobbler was concerned, because he was supposed to help us solve a big case. He did, and gave us the information we needed. In return, we let him off scot-free for a little fencing we could hardly have proved him guilty of anyway."

"Yes, Carl must have found out," Rona continued. "He was afraid Nobbler would inform on him again. He'd hired Williams as the driver of the car used in Susan Kelford's abduction. Carl, however, hadn't told Nobbler Williams beforehand that it was a child abduction. Williams, however, wanted nothing to do with it. He strongly reproached Knight after the fact. So Knight had every reason to fear revelations from Nobbler."

"In fact, Nobbler Williams did contact Scotland Yard and summoned us to a pub in Chatham to talk to him," Houston said. "But what did Knight say about the yellow windmill, Rona?"

"He had set out to kidnap Susan Kelford in order to blackmail her father into paying a ransom. Then he realised that he needed something that would attract the child's attention and win Susan over. An unusual toy would be best, he thought. He remembered the yellow windmill in Dr Spedro's consulting room. He got himself a copy of the same model. He also intended, of course..."

"...to throw suspicion on to Dr Spedro," Houston remembered. "He knew that if we could identify the car, we would come across Dr Spedro and pay him a visit. In doing so, we had to notice the windmill in the doctor's consulting room, and automatically, so to speak, the doctor would seem suspicious to us."

Rona nodded. "That's how he had it figured out."

"He seems to have thought of everything in the first place," Houston growled grimly. "And you think he was telling the truth about Dennis?"

"I really believe him, Dad. Why would he have lied to me? Remember, he asked for me to visit him in hospital. I'm sure he wouldn't have done that if..."

"You're right," Houston said. "I just wanted to hear again if you were quite sure he was speaking honestly. There's something else that makes me think his statement was true."

Rona didn't ask him what it was. Suddenly she realised that he was driving towards Eaton Square.

"I must speak to Sir Cedric Kelford at once," Houston explained to her as she inquired in surprise where they were going.

"What now? At this hour?"

"Yes," Houston reaffirmed his decision. "An hour earlier or later might be crucial now."

***

The first pale glow of dawn was gathering over London as Houston pressed the bell button on Kelford's house.

He didn't have to wait long. Kelford fended off the Inspector's excuses. "I'm an early riser, Inspector. You don't have to worry about disturbing me. I have the best thoughts and ideas quite early in the morning."

He led them into a small dining room. "May I invite you to join me in having some breakfast?"

"I'd love a coffee," Houston said. "There won't be time to eat anything. I'm in a great hurry, Sir Cedric. But I have a few important questions I'd like to talk to you about."

He opened his briefcase, took out some papers from it and handed them to the bank president. Sir Cedric glanced at them. A quiet exclamation escaped him. With a jerk, he raised his head and looked at Houston.

"Do you know what this is, Inspector? Photocopies of the plans for a new nuclear power plant that a private industrial group close to us wants to build. We knew that information about this project had been leaked to the competition. We have been trying for some time to clarify how this indiscretion could have happened."

Houston had taken a quick sip of coffee. "The original papers are still in the bank's possession, aren't they?"

Sir Cedric nodded. "Of course. I can vouch for that."

"In what way was the information about these plans valuable to outsiders?" inquired Houston.

Kelford pushed his plate aside and leaned forward. "We became suspicious when we realised that someone on the stock exchange was trying to buy up large blocks of shares in our group. We watched the manoeuvre and very quickly realised that it was the competition that was trying to get its foot in the door of our company, so to speak. So the others had to know what we were planning."

Houston nodded. "I see." Sir Cedric hesitated for a moment before asking, "Can you tell me who you got these copies from?"

"They were in the possession of one of your former employees – Bob Harridge. He was with us a few hours ago. On that occasion he inadvertently took my briefcase and left his. The young man never struck me as quite house-broken lately. His interest in the progress of the investigation seemed a little too strong to be considered normal. I suspected something. And that's why I took the liberty of examining his bag earlier. That's where I found these papers. By the way," he smiled, "I couldn't swear that I didn't arrange the mix-up of the two bags..."

"Dad, you don't think...?"

Houston fended off Rona's attempt to interrupt him by speaking quickly on, "Harridge will surely have discovered the loss of the documents by now. That is the reason, Sir Cedric, that I visit you at this unusual hour. You will admit we have no time to lose."

Rona looked from one to the other. "Only what has all this to do with Dennis's death?"

Her father pointed to the photocopies. "I'm sure Dennis was murdered because of these papers."

Rona's eyes widened. "You mean Bob Harridge killed him..."

She saw her father nod mutely.

Dismayed, she stammered, "I don't know what to think anymore. First Carl a multiple murderer! A kidnapper! And now Bob – he was always so nice to me, and I thought he and Dennis were friends. I..."

She broke off and jumped up. Sobbing, she went out.

156

Sir Cedric hurried after her, opened the door, pointed out and whispered something to Rona.

"I was just telling her to lie down for a bit," he explained as he returned to the table. "All this must have taken a terrible toll on her."

Houston had risen to his feet. "Thank you, Sir Cedric." He reached for his briefcase. "I must be going. There is much to be done."

Kelford accompanied him to the front door. "One more thing, Inspector," he said half aloud. "I didn't want to mention it earlier in Rona's presence. We have investigated the indiscretion affair very carefully. There is no doubt that Dennis was involved in it along with Bob Harridge."

Houston bowed his head. "I thank you very much for telling me that, Sir Cedric."

"You won't mention any of this to Rona, will you?" inquired Sir Cedric anxiously. "She was very fond of her brother and has been through enough lately."

"You are very considerate."

"Not at all, I'm just infinitely in her debt. Beyond that, I admire her a lot. She's a great girl with more character than many have. It would hurt me very much if she were hurt any more."

***

On the way back to the Yard, Houston realised a few things. Somehow Dennis had got hold of those photocopies and then had hesitated to hand them over to Bob Harridge. Perhaps he had even thought of destroying them or handing them over to the police. Obviously, however, Harridge had been determined to prevent that at all costs.

He had come by that fatal evening when Dennis was home alone to watch Rona's play on TV. He asked for the photocopies, which Dennis refused to hand over. After killing Dennis, Harridge had scratched the yellow windmill on the television, correctly assuming that the murder would be linked to the crimes committed by Carl Knight. Then he'd searched Dennis's room but couldn't find the photocopies. They were hidden in the secret compartment Dennis had cut into Mrs Spedro's book. Later, Harridge had returned and entered the flat to search Dennis's room again. Rona had surprised him. And again he'd had to leave without what he had come for.

Since the murder, he had repeatedly appeared at Houston's flat. Ostensibly out of interest in Rona. In reality, however, he wanted to explore a favourable opportunity for a new search and at the same time keep up to date with the state of the investigation.

At Scotland Yard, Houston immediately requested an arrest warrant for Bob Harridge. He found the young man's address on a business card Harridge had given him after setting up his brokerage firm.

***

Shortly after seven in the morning, Houston rang the bell at the house where Harridge lived. The building was surrounded by police officers.

He had to wait a minute before the door was opened. An elderly woman with upturned hair looked at him disapprovingly. The rollers on her head bobbed. "Bob Harridge? He's not here. Five minutes at the most since he left the house."

Houston had to stifle a curse. "Do you have any idea where he was going?"

"No sir, he packed his things, paid up and drove away."

"In his car?"

"No, he sold it two days ago. In a taxi."

Houston let himself be driven to the next taxi rank. He was lucky. One of the three drivers standing waiting recalled that a call had come from the street where Harridge lived.

"The person in question was going to Victoria Station. Perhaps that's the man you're looking for, sir."

At Victoria Station, Houston jumped out of the car and ran up to a porter and grabbed him by the arm.

"Which train is leaving next?"

The man looked at him in confusion, caught himself and said, "To Dover, sir – platform six." Houston left him standing and waved to the policemen who had accompanied him. "Search all the platforms! I'll take platform six."

He ran through the barrier, past the baffled ticket collector.

The train to Dover began to move slowly. Houston caught a compartment door of the last carriage, yanked it open and swung himself inside. He walked along the corridor, looking through each compartment window and musing at the faces of the passengers. When he reached the third carriage, a compartment door slid aside, someone tried to step out and retreated back into the compartment in a flash.

Bob Harridge...

In two leaps Houston was at the door and pushed it open. Harridge was alone. He stared at the Inspector.

"You'd better stay out, Houston!" he groaned hotly.

"Don't be a fool, Harridge!" growled Houston. "Don't think you can get away from us. You haven't got a chance now."

Harridge's hand went into his trouser pocket.

"You're not making it easy for me, Inspector."

Houston looked into the muzzle of a revolver. He sprang forward, got hold of Harridge's right arm and pushed it up. Harridge was so surprised that the revolver fell from his hand. Gasping, Houston pushed him against the window. The train rumbled over a switch, making the carriage lurch back and forth. Harridge wrenched an arm from its grasp and slammed Houston against his left temple.

The Inspector slumped to the bench, Harridge on top of him. Houston struggled violently. He came halfway up, but a blow threw him back on the bench. Harridge bent down to pick up the revolver. Houston made a tremendous effort. Gasping, they wrestled. The Inspector realised that his strength was failing. Harridge was twenty years younger than him. A fist crashed against Houston's chin. Then he sank back into the seat. Harridge holstered the revolver and smoothed his hair. Almost subconsciously, Houston heard the other man push open the compartment door. A breeze brushed his face. Mechanically, he grabbed Harridge's leg and tugged. But the other freed himself and hurried out. Houston scrambled to his feet, held on to the doorframe and looked into the corridor. Harridge had reached the end of the corridor and opened the outer door. The train had slowed down. Before Houston could call out, Bob Harridge jumped....

At the next station, the Inspector left the train as fast as he could. Every step caused him pain. His skull throbbed. But the orders he gave over the stationmaster's phone were clear. An hour later, a small search party found Bob Harridge. He was lying in a hedge at the foot of the high railway embankment. His neck was broken.

***

Silently, Mike Houston allowed Sir Cedric Kelford to pour him a second glass of whisky. He sat in front of the fireplace in Kelford's sitting room and watched as in one corner Rona played with little Susan.

"You must be feeling very relieved now that it's all over," Kelford said, raising his glass.

"Yes," Houston nodded. "It's a load off my mind, I can tell you. I've been worried about Rona in particular lately. But now she can get back to her theatre work without any excitement."

160

Rona had stepped behind him as he spoke and sat on the arm of the chair.

"That's the least of my worries," she interjected with a smile, squeezing his arm. For the first time he noticed that she was wearing a diamond ring. Houston raised his head slowly, looking from Rona to Kelford, from Kelford to Rona.

"What's going on here?" he asked.

Rona laughed.

"Everything's fine, Inspector," she assured him with a quizzical look in her eyes. "I'm taking on a whole new role soon – that's all..."

THE END

AFTERWORD
by Dr. Georg Pagitz

Francis Durbridge's novels are mainly based on his radio
scripts, film and television scripts, which were usually written
into book form by a ghostwriter. This was also the case, for
example, with his first five novels, all of which were based on
radio plays with Paul Temple.

A special exception is Durbridge's sixth novel, *Back
Room Girl*, which was published in 1950 and has never been
translated into German. It is the only one of the author's
criminal novels that does not follow the whodunit pattern and
in which the perpetrator is known from the beginning. It is
also more of an exciting adventure story in which a former
major and a female scientist fight against a dangerous
organisation consisting of brutal Nazis who want to impose
world domination with a nuclear missile. Although James
Bond did not exist in 1950, this story sounds more like 007
than Durbridge. World domination fantasies moved the globe
at the time. Durbridge unusually for him shows a lot of
violence, which in turn is carried out by the extremely brutal
ex-Nazis. The title *Back Room Girl* refers to the female main
character Karen Silvers, who works on a secret government
project behind closed doors, sealed off from the outside
world, in a "back room" as it were. Although untypical for the
author, the story is exciting and offers some interesting twists.
Moreover, the old monastery, from which various secret
passages lead away (including a pub), is clearly a borrowing
from Durbridge's model Edgar Wallace.

After this novel, Durbridge launched *Beware of Johnny
Washington* in 1951, a rewrite of his first novel *Send for Paul
Temple* from 1938 (German translation: *Paul Temple und der
Fall Max Lorraine*, 2021, Pidax). The eighth novel, *Design
for Murder* (*Mr. Rossiter Recommends Himself*, or,

162

respectively, *Kind Regards from Mr. Brix*), was a reworking of another Temple adventure.

In the early to mid-1950s, Durbridge concentrated on writing a number of serial novels for magazines, in addition to his constant television and radio work and his ongoing involvement in cinema adaptations and the Temple comic series.

In 1952/1953 *The Nylon Murders* appeared in the *Sunday Dispatch* as a twelve-part serial (in the German book versions *Kommt Zeit, kommt Mord* and *Die Nylonmorde*).

Francis Durbridge published his tenth novel, *The Yellow Windmill*, as an eleven-part serial, also in the *Sunday Dispatch* in 1954. Like the following novel *The Man Who Beat the Panel* (1955 in *TV Mirror*), German version as *Mitten ins Hertz* in *Bild und Funk* (1962/1963), and the fifteenth novel *The Face of Carol West*, German version as *Sie wussten zuviel* in *Bild und Funk* (1963), this novel appeared in Germany in TV magazines.

What is special about it is that the perfectionist Francis Durbridge revises the stories, expands them considerably, changes names, motifs, places, length and number of episodes (*Panel* has six episodes in the English version, nine in the German, *Carol West* has eight episodes in the original and ten in the German version) and, in the case of *The Man Who Beat the Panel*, makes a whodunit out of a non-whodunit, while also introducing new characters here and changing the nature of the criminal organisation and its crimes.

For *The Yellow Windmill* it should be said that the German version translated here, which appeared in *Bild und Funk* in the winter of 1965/1966, differs greatly from the English version, especially at the beginning, and in some cases also has different character names.

The further the story progresses, the more similar the two versions become. Durbridge seems to have been particularly

163

unhappy with the beginning of the original English version, otherwise he would hardly have revised it.

Melvyn Barnes, author of *Francis Durbridge: The Complete Guide* **(Williams & Whiting, 2018), completes this volume with a Francis Durbridge survey –**

My friend Georg Pagitz has written an informative Introduction to this translation of one of Francis Durbridge's German magazine serials. But for those not entirely familiar with the master thriller-writer's life and career, this brief article puts Durbridge into crime fiction context and shows him to be a multi-media playwright whose name is most unlikely to fade.

Francis Henry Durbridge was born into a middle-class family in Kingston upon Hull on 25 November 1912. His parents were Francis and Gertrude Durbridge, his father being a Woolworths store manager who rose to control the store's Midland region. Francis junior married Norah Elizabeth Lawley in 1940 and they had two sons, Stephen (who became a literary agent) and Nicholas (who became a specialist in copyright law and product licensing).

He was educated at Bradford Grammar School, Wylde Green College and Birmingham University, and while an undergraduate he decided to pursue his schoolboy ambition to become a writer. Already, as a teenager, he had written a play called *The Great Dutton* which was performed for charity. The bug had clearly bitten, and although he spent a brief period in a stockbroker's office his career as a full-time writer was launched by the British Broadcasting Corporation in the early 1930s with his children's stories, comedy plays, musical libretti and numerous short sketches. While his earliest airing was a play called *The Three-Cornered Hat* in *The Children's Hour* on the BBC Midland Region on 25 July 1933, his radio dramas *Promotion* (1934), *Murder in the Midlands* (1934) and *Murder in the Embassy* (1937) stood out from his otherwise light-hearted output and indicated the direction he was ultimately to follow.

In 1938 Durbridge established himself as a crime writer in particular, several months before his twenty-sixth birthday, when the BBC Midland Region broadcast his serial *Send for Paul Temple*. The listening public submitted over 7,000 requests for more, and he rapidly became one of the foremost writers of radio thrillers. The Durbridge dream team of novelist/detective Paul Temple and his wife Steve was thoroughly launched, with the 1938 *Paul Temple and the Front Page Men* followed by another twenty-six Paul Temple mysteries until 1968 of which seven were new productions of earlier cases.

In the mid-twentieth century radio detectives were extremely popular, and Paul Temple's rivals included Dick Barton (by Edward J. Mason), Philip Odell (by Lester Powell), Dr. Morelle (by Ernest Dudley), P.C. 49 (by Alan Stranks) and Ambrose West (by Philip Levene). In fact in the 1940s, in addition to the Temples, Durbridge wrote radio dramas featuring investigators called Anthony Sherwood, Johnny Cordell, Amanda Smith, Gail Carlton, Michael Starr, André d'Arnell and Johnny Washington, and he even wrote a radio serial featuring the legendary Sexton Blake.

The Paul Temple radio serials acquired a massive European following, with translated versions broadcast in the Netherlands from 1939 (*Spreek met Vlaanderen en het komt in orde / Send for Paul Temple*), Germany from 1949 (*Paul Temple und die Affäre Gregory / Paul Temple and the Gregory Affair*), Italy from 1953 (*Paul Temple, il romanziere poliziotto / A Case for Paul Temple*) and Denmark from 1954 (*Gregory mysteriet / Paul Temple and the Gregory Affair*). And in his own country Temple was adopted as the daily hero of a long-running syndicated newspaper strip from 1950 to 1971.

Then in 1952, while continuing to write for radio, Durbridge embarked on a long sequence of BBC television serials that achieved enormous viewing figures until 1980. Although his reputation from 1938 onwards had rested on the regular radio exploits of the Temples, it was his parallel television career from the 1950s that firmly established his name – with gripping serials including *Portrait of Alison, My Friend Charles, The Scarf, The World of Tim Frazer, Melissa, A Man Called Harry Brent* and *Bat out of Hell*. And again in Europe his television serials proved phenomenally popular, beginning in Germany with *Der Andere / The Other Man* (1959), in Sweden with *Halsduken / The Scarf* (1962), in Finland with *Huivi / The Scarf* (1962), in Italy with *La Sciarpa / The Scarf* (1963), in France with *L'écharpe / The Scarf* (1966) and in Poland with *Szal / The Scarf* (1970).

In the UK his appeal on the small screen was unrivalled, with the result that for all his serials from 1960 (beginning with *The World of Tim Frazer*) the BBC gave him the unprecedented accolade of the "Francis Durbridge Presents" screen credit before the title sequence of each episode. But there was a third string to his bow, as from 1971 in the UK and even earlier in Germany he wrote for the theatrical stage and became known for intriguing twist-after-twist plots, with such plays as *Suddenly at Home, Murder with Love* and *House Guest*.

Many of Durbridge's radio and television serials were novelised from 1938 to 1988 and frequently reprinted, numerous Paul Temple radio serials were marketed as CDs, and his television serials from *The Desperate People* (1963) to *Breakaway* (1980) were all released in 2016 as DVDs. There were also nine cinema films in the 1940s and 1950s derived from his radio and television serials, which much later became available on DVDs – *Send for Paul Temple, Calling Paul Temple, Paul Temple's Triumph, Paul Temple Returns*,

167

The Broken Horseshoe, Operation Diplomat, The Teckman Mystery, Portrait of Alison and *The Vicious Circle.*

Francis Durbridge died on 11 April 1998 in Barnes, a leafy area outside London that had been his home and the milieu that had become so familiar in his plots. Radio and television stations in Germany were particularly glowing in their obituaries and in their praise for his work, describing his serials as unforgettable masterpieces and recalling the days when Durbridge cliff-hangers resulted in deserted German streets because a huge majority of the population stayed at home, glued to their radios and television sets.

In all, he was an icon of popular culture who deserves to be remembered.

Printed in Great Britain
by Amazon